Champion
Bubbler

A novel

JULES MITCHELL BAILEY

ISBN-13: 978-1511942010

ISBN-10: 1511942010

Printed and bound in the United States of America

Printed by CreateSpace

First paperback edition June 2015
Revised May 2016

Cover designed by Tehuti Ra

DEDICATION

Dedicated to all the people living in the ghetto:
Young girls struggling to find a way out;
Young boys looking for a role model;
Mothers trying to find ways to take care of their fatherless children;
Fathers who will do whatever it takes to provide for their families!

ACKNOWLEDGMENTS

Many thanks for the support of my family: my husband, Leeroy Bailey; my children, Romaine, Roshaine and LeeAnne. To my sister, Jennifer Brown, who graciously took the time to review this book and provide feedback. I truly appreciate your help. To my wonderful friend, Shamiso Barnett, for listening as I rumbled on and on about Bubbler and for taking the time to provide edits and feedback. Your support is invaluable. To my awesome co-workers and first critics, Dorna Werdelin and Nicole Johnson, who encouraged me to get this book published. You ladies are my rock! Dorna, thanks also for your proofreading skills and insightful intellect. To my friend, Martin Langdon, for his support and assistance.

To all the wonderful people reading this book—a heartfelt thanks in advance! I hope you enjoy reading this story as much as I enjoyed writing it.

Champion
Bubbler

CHAPTER ONE

They didn't call me Bubbler for nothing. Momma said the first day I got up off the floor to walk I shook my ass like I was a pro. I haven't stopped shaking my ass since. I was born to be an exotic dancer. On Friday and Saturday nights, the bar down the street in the ghetto neighborhood in Kingston where we lived played a jukebox outside on the corner, and I would draw a crowd. The owner didn't care because it meant more business for him. Momma didn't care because she was too busy scheming and chasing after one of her many sugar daddies.

I don't even know who my father is. Some people said it was the man from the countryside who used to sell yam in the open-air market on the weekends. Others said it was the man who lived with his wife and five children across the main road, but frequently visited our house. Still others said it was the bus driver who would park the long passenger bus in front of our yard on every break he took from work. He vexed a lot of our neighbors because he was always blocking someone's driveway and when they tried to get him to move the bus, Mr. Bus Driver wouldn't leave out of that house until he got ready to. It didn't matter how loud our neighbors called Momma's name or beat down our front door, they would have to wait.

We lived in a big house that was sectioned off and rented out to different families. Some called a living situation like this "tenement yard" while others said "big yard." Momma rented a side portion of the house with one bedroom, a small living area and a kitchen. We used the bathroom and toilet at the back of the house that everyone used. Sometimes it was a shuffle to get in the bathroom in the mornings so the children usually bathed in a wash tub outside in the yard. Even the grown-ups bathed outside too at nights.

Our landlady loved Momma. She always said that Momma was the only tenant she didn't have to track down at the beginning of the month when it was time to collect rent. Momma would have her money ready. She also took very good care of her portion of the house and she would have one of her sugar daddies paint and fix it up every Christmas before she put out decorations and Christmas lights.

I don't even know what my real name was. I've never seen my birth certificate. When I turned 18 and asked Momma for it she cursed me out.

"Don't ask me any questions. Because you feel that you are a grown woman now you think you can just come up into my yard demanding shit from me? Girl, get the hell outta here!" she shouted at me.

I never asked her about my birth certificate after that. I was registered in school as Ethel Long and that's what they all called me, but I hated that damn name. It made me sound like a retarded old woman. So when I got older, I started calling myself Mercedes Ford. I merged two car names together and swore upside down that I was going to own one or the other. I just needed to play my cards right and attract the right sugar daddy.

All our neighbors talked about Momma, but she didn't care. She said they were just jealous and that they weren't helping her to pay her rent and take care of her bills. Although they talked behind her back, they were too afraid to face her. She always had her pocket knife and a bottle of acid in her handbag and she was not afraid to use them. She had seen a lot of things going down in our depressed neighborhood so she was not scared of anyone or anything.

Her daddy was the area leader and everyone called him Dan Daddy. He had influence over politicians and controlled the public work issued by the government. He also controlled the women in his community. My mother had two sisters born to different mothers the same year she was born. The women used to fight over my granddaddy and they were always in competition with each other for his attention. He was always dapper and when he walked into a dancehall show everyone moved out of his way to let him pass.

Granddaddy had gotten so powerful that he started to disrespect the other men in the community. He would openly flirt with their women in their presence and by the end of the dancehall show the women would be leaving their men to spend the night with him. He was greasing their men's palms so they couldn't show him any screw face. Most of the dudes in the neighborhood were sick and tired of him, but no one had the gall to challenge him. No one of course until he crossed Little Bandit's path.

Everyone knew my granddaddy was messing with Little Bandit's lady friend. Little Bandit would go to the dance with her and she would disappear on him. Word on the street was that my granddaddy would have his driver pick her up and take her to his crib and Little Bandit wouldn't see her until the next day.

Little Bandit's daddy was my granddaddy's best friend, but he took the fall for my granddaddy on a corruption charge that had all evidence pointing to him and not my granddaddy. He was spending 20 years to life in prison and my granddaddy promised that he would take care of Little Bandit, but he never did anything for the kid. Little Bandit grew up around the older boys and ended up running the streets and selling weed.

So one night after my granddaddy left the dancehall, Little Bandit approached him and in a split second put a bullet straight through his head. He walked out swinging his gun like the gangster he was. Everyone in the dance saw Little Bandit shoot my granddaddy, but it didn't matter how much pressure the cops laid down, no one would snitch. In a way a lot of people were happy that my granddaddy was taken out.

Grandma would talk about how his funeral was like a state affair with police escorts and all. Granddaddy's casket was placed in a glass-covered carriage drawn by two white horses as it paraded around the neighborhood with his brother in the driver's seat.

"It was something to see; he went out in style," my grandmother boasted.

My cousins and I had heard this story so many times, but each time Grandma told it, she seemed to add more information.

"The road was lined with people craning their necks to get a good look at him lying in that casket. He was just as handsome in death as he was in real life. I loved that man so much I would give anything to lie next to him in that casket," she sighed.

"Yuck," my little cousin said. "Why would you want to lie next to someone who is dead? Grandma, that sounds like someone who is crazy."

"When you are young and in love you do and think some crazy things. Y'all just wait and see," she told us.

"Is that the reason why you threw yourself across the casket in the church and wouldn't let go?" I asked.

"Nope, that was not me at all. Whosoever told you that is lying. It was Pinky," my grandmother said referring to one of granddaddy's other baby mothers.

"And who would not let the undertakers close the grave because she hung on to the side and would not let go?" my cousin asked.

"That was Marcia," my grandmother said referring to another baby mother. "She told them if they try to remove her she was going to jump inside the grave with the casket. They had to wait until she calmed down to cover the hole. I didn't do anything crazy. I was his main woman and so all attention was on me and the limousine that my girls and I rode in. I didn't have to seek any attention by acting crazy."

"So Grandma, you didn't cry one bit?" my cousin asked.

"Yeah I cried. But my tears fell behind my sunglasses. I was too fly to have tears rolling all over messing up my new outfit and my makeup. I had my white handkerchief blotting my face like the movie stars do," she said with her hand mimicking the movement while she held her head up high.

We all laughed.

Momma was a little girl when her daddy got killed and so she didn't get the chance to really know him. But everyone said she grew up to look just like him and had the same cold and cruel heart as he did. So no one would mess with Momma; she was a bad bitch. Momma would also dress her ass off and everything had to be tight–her shoes, handbags, garments and jewelry. She never left home without putting on her face–her makeup was to die for. And don't even mention her hairstyle–it looked as if she woke up in the hairdresser's chair every morning. Momma didn't wear anything that was cheap. If she wasn't shopping in New Kingston, she would have her friends bring her garments when they went to the islands of Curacao and Panama.

As much as Momma had her sugar daddies showering her with gifts and money, she still worked. She usually said that she needed to have something extra in case someone didn't show up. Momma used to work at the Freezone Factory as a machine operator and met a man who was working as a customs officer at the Wharf. He was giving Momma all kinds of gifts and very soon she claimed she "fell in love" and he moved in with us. After my mother's lover, Andre, moved in with us, Momma stopped having other men coming to the house so the neighbors didn't have anything to talk about anymore. She had become a "lady" overnight. Andre bought her a big ass diamond ring that she wore on her wedding finger.

∞∞∞

I was still going around the street to dance to music

every Friday and Saturday night. There were several young girls who would join me and we would compete with each other. None of them had the size ass that I had or could shake theirs like I shook mine; thus, I was always the star of the show.

One night Andre came to the bar and when he saw me dancing he stopped to look. I put on a performance that night. By the time I reached home, my mother was at the gate waiting for me. She had never gotten vex before when she saw me dance or heard how I "turned it up." She had even laughed a few times with the other women in the yard about this.

"Pearl, that daughter of yours is no joke. You should see how she threw that ass up into the air as the music started playing. She made the grown ass women look like they weren't trying. I think the girls around here wish they had her ass," one of the women said.

"I know. I remember how it was when I was younger. They used to be so jealous of me," my Momma said laughing.

"She has a money maker right there," the woman said referring to my ass.

But that night Momma told me that I could not go around there anymore because it made Andre uncomfortable and it was not "ladylike." She now wanted to turn me into the "lady" she had become overnight.

Andre did not waste any time in knocking Momma up. After she got pregnant, she was so sick that she couldn't go to work and eventually they fired her for not showing up. Andre started doting on Momma and would give her all the attention she wanted. He would rub her belly and put his head on it as if he was listening to hear something. He would get her anything she needed and Momma was enjoying all the attention.

"Babe, I feel for some fish tea soup. Babe, I feel for some boiled corn. Babe, I feel for some jerk chicken. Babe, I feel for some green mangoes …" and the list went on. Momma was all of a sudden feeling for everything and Andre would run out and get it for her. They killed me with their "honey" and "babe" all the time. Momma did not pay me any attention anymore and I became jealous of their relationship so I tried to make it hell for Andre living with us. I quickly grew up and in no time graduated from high school and was not around them much anymore.

After graduating from high school, all I did was roam the streets and entertain a host of "sugar daddies." My mother could not afford to send me to college and I wasn't interested either so after a few years of not doing anything with my life, I ended up dancing at a strip club right after my 21st birthday. One day my childhood friend, Trina, and I met a dude in New Kingston and he told us he owned a club in Montego Bay and was looking for "look good girls" like us to dance. We went home, packed our bags and told our folks that we were leaving. We boarded a mini-bus to Montego Bay and never looked back.

CHAPTER
TWO

"Shake that ass Bubbler ... yeah ... shake that ass," was all I heard every time I took the stage. I loved hearing the men when they squealed and hee-hawed over my sexy ass. I had their minds all wrapped up into me and I was not even touching them. I knew I had them jacking off in their pants and it made me feel in control. That's how it was for me and my German sugar daddy, Greg. I was sitting on the beach one day when he approached me and asked me where he could get some action.

"What kind of action are you looking for?" I asked. "Sex? Weed? What is it you are trying to get?"

He looked at me; laughed and said, "I wouldn't mind getting some ass like yours."

Although I was making a pile of cash every night dancing at a strip club, I didn't turn away any business. Girls needed to look fly all the time and fashionable wears were expensive too, so I took him to my crib. I removed my sundress but before I could take off my panties, he ejaculated. The embarrassment on his face was so evident–he turned beet red. I had never been with a White dude before and I was curious.

"That's okay," I said, "You can just pay me now; business is business."

Without saying anything, he handed me some U.S. dollars and left. Two days later, I ran into him walking along the beach and he tried to look away. I ran up to him and said, "Hey, are you looking for some more action?" He laughed and shook his head. We started walking and talking and I was really feeling his conversation and asked if he wanted to join me for lunch. We walked over to a shack along the roadside where fried fish was being sold and bought a plate full and sat down to eat.

I was all up into his business asking him what he was doing in Jamaica and if he was alone or came with a family.

"No, I am alone on vacation," he told me.

"Are you having fun?" I asked.

"Yeah, I am just relaxing. I am not into a whole lot, just enjoying the beach and the food."

"What about the liquor and some weed? We have the real deal here."

He laughed. "I do some of that too."

"You need an island girl to hang with now to complete your vacation," I instigated.

He flashed me a boyish smile and his green eyes caught my attention. I had never been up so close to anyone with green eyes before and I thought they looked great against his tanned skin. I couldn't stop myself as I muttered, "Your eyes are so stunning."

He blushed, looked away and said, "I was thinking the

same about your skin. It looks so …" he paused as if trying to find the right words then said, "smooth and silky."

The next time Greg and I hooked up at my place, I flipped my ass on the bed ready for him. I was anxious to see if it felt any different from the Black dudes I was accustomed to. He backed off his shirt and dropped his pants and underwear on the floor. His body was lean and muscular with hairs covering his entire chest. As he headed toward the bed he had a look of confidence about him that he didn't have the first time he was at my place. I knew he was ready to show me what he had going on, but I was ready to have him begging me for more. He had me quivering and I was so shocked. I had never had any dude made me feel like that before. How did he do that? I wondered. When he was finally through with me, I laid my ass on the bed and told him to just lock the door when he got ready to leave.

So after his three weeks' vacation on the island ended and several more hookups, Greg gave me his number in Germany and told me to call him anytime I wanted to.

∞∞∞∞

Five of us worked at the club stripping on rotation. I had a sexy ass with a pair of breasts that were round and firm that every dude wanted to fondle and suck. My tiny waistline made both my ass and breasts seem even more delicious, and dudes drooled over my chocolate-brown body. I loved the attention and I loved the stage. I knew how to control all the men with the movements of my body as I danced.

When my friend, Trina, and I first arrived the other girls immediately started hating on us. They would eye us suspiciously and whenever they were grouped up talking, the conversation would end as soon as we walked by. They gave us dirty looks or said some funny jokes to each other as if they were talking in codes.

"To hell with dem," Trina would say. "We are here to make money not to make friends."

"Yeah girl let's shake that booty and pile up that dough," I chanted.

"These back-bushes, country fools can't measure up to us. We are from Kingston, baby," I laughed.

Trina had big plans—she wanted to go to cosmetology school and own her own hairdressing business. She said she headed to Montego Bay with me to dance in the club because she was tired of seeing her mother struggling to take care of her and her brothers and sisters and she had no interest into going to college. We went to the same primary school, but she had passed her exam to go to one of the prominent high schools uptown, while I went to a local high school in our area. We saw each other all the time because we would still hang out after school and on the weekends. Her Pops was so proud of her when she passed her exam that he boasted to everyone in the area his daughter was going to go to college to study to be a doctor or a lawyer.

"Doctor Trina," I would tease her.

"He can say anything he wants to say. I am going to own my salon uptown," was what she always said.

She had a natural talent for doing hair and could hook up any hair style: braids, cornrows, African twists, relaxers; you name it, Trina could do it. Sometimes she had her clientele hanging out on her verandah patiently waiting to get their hair done.

Trina's father was in charge of the mailroom operations at a government agency in Kingston. He collapsed at work and died on the stretcher on his way into surgery. He had a heart attack. So after her father passed and her mother was forced to work, Trina had to take care of her sister and four younger brothers and didn't have any free time to do hair anymore.

When Trina told her mother she was leaving Kingston with me, her mother was furious. "You need a college education. Without a good education all you are going to do is to live like a lowlife. Look at me Trina, do you think this was the life I wanted? I didn't have a jack soul who cared so I had to leave the countryside to find work. Your father was a good man–Lord bless his soul! He wanted the best for you all and since he is not here I am working to carry out his wishes. I want the best for you Trina," she told her.

"I understand Mom but I can't stay here any longer and watch you work like a dog," she said. So she packed her bags and headed out with me.

∞∞∞∞

One night at the club, Trina and I went in early to chill before it was time for our act. The owner, Danny, usually had us working back-to-back and sometimes we would do our acts together on stage. As we sat in the back lounge area chilling with some dudes, one of the other girls who danced at the club passed by the table and shot us a dirty look. One of the dudes was really up into my face, but I was so used to being the center of attention that his presence did not faze me. We were just kicking back and having a good time chatting.

When we went backstage to change, the girl who shot us the dirty look attacked me. She was standing in the doorway with the other two girls obviously waiting for us. She caught me off guard and knocked me out cold with a piece of iron pipe. It landed across my head and the dudes in charge of the sound system poured water over me to revive me. When I regained consciousness, my attacker had flashed out the door and was nowhere in sight. I told her friends that I was going to beat her ass the next time she came to the club, but she never returned. I found out that the dude who was all up into my face was sleeping with her and she hit me in a jealous rage.

Several weeks passed and I almost forgot the incident when I ran into the girl in town. When she saw me she tried to run, but I grabbed her and started punching her. She was kicking, screaming and biting at me, as we stumbled on the ground. I got on top of her and started throwing punches all over her face. Someone pulled me off her and when she got up I tore her clothes off her leaving her in underwear. I continued to beat the crap out of her until she fell down on the ground. A crowd had gathered and a man picked her up and put her in the back seat of a taxi and took her to the hospital. After word got around to the other two girls, they never looked at Trina and me that way again. We were at the club to do a job and that's what we did.

CHAPTER THREE

I stretched out on the lounge chair on the balcony of the condo I was renting as I sipped on a bottle of Red Stripe Beer. I had planned on going downtown to the nail salon to get my nails done, but I did not feel like doing anything. All morning I sprawled around in my pajamas. Looking out at the sea, it looked calm and peaceful and as usual there were people musing around on the beach. I had only been in Montego Bay for a few months and already I was living in style. This was so far removed from when Trina and I first got there. When we came off the mini-bus that day in town, we had no plans and did not know where we were staying.

We had walked around until we saw a motel. It was an hourly paid one, but I sweet-talked the attendant on duty into giving us a room on a weekly rate. By the time I was done buttering him up, we ended up with two rooms for a fixed-rate. I even suggested that if he needed some action I would take care of him for free. Walking to the rooms, Trina said, "Bubbler you are something else. You are such a God damn trick! How did you learn to be so smooth with men?"

"I got it from Momma. Remember, everyone knows she was up on her game," I said.

"And she got it from her Poppa," Trina said laughing.

I learned a lot by just watching how my Momma operated, and I had become a pro at handling myself and smooth-talking men to get my way. At the motel, I was happy that we had our own rooms, because Trina was not into the games I was playing–she was a good girl. She only lost her virginity to a Chinese dude, Chris, who she thought she was in love with just before we left Kingston to work in the club. His family owned the meat mart on the main road, but they kept within their own groups and would not have accepted Chris going out with Trina. She had been secretively having sex with him without using any protection and then one day she came crying to me, "Bubbler, I think I am pregnant."

"What?" I shouted.

"Stop joking with me. I thought you said you weren't allowing any man to get close to you because you are going to be a nun," I joked.

Looking at me with a straight face and ignoring my joke she said, "Chris cum inside of me yesterday and I just know I am pregnant. Momma is going to kill me," she wailed.

I realized then how serious the situation was so I stopped joking around. Unsure of what to say I stood looking at her.

Trina continued, "What am I going to do Bubbler? My mother said if I go out and breed I can't stay here. She cannot afford to feed another mouth and I know Chris' parents won't take me in."

She looked at me as if her life depended on what I had to

say. I told her it was too early to tell so she had to wait until her cycle and if it did not come, I would follow her down to the clinic.

"You are a grown ass woman now. If you are pregnant you just have to get your own place and let Chris take care of you," I told her.

Every day Trina bawled and stressed me out about being pregnant so after the third week of her nagging, I followed her to the clinic to get a pregnancy test done. When she found out it was negative, she told the nurse to put her on the injection. So after that Trina was giving Chris all the sex he wanted and he was showering her with all kind of gifts.

Chris was upset when Trina told him that she was leaving for Montego Bay with me. "You are going down there with her to sell your crotch. That's it, right?" he shouted.

"No Chris, I am not like that. You know that too. She got a job dancing in a club and I am going to work as the bartender," she said. So that's the story we told before we left home. Everyone knew that I loved dancing so it did not come as a surprise that I would want to dance in a club.

We had put the money we earned together and rented a two bedroom house and moved out of the motel. Trina thought that Chris could now come to visit whenever he was able to. But about a month after we left, Chris told Trina that he was going out with the Indian girl who lived across the main road. Her daddy owned the liquor store and was well known in the area. He said his parents liked her and thought they were perfect for each other. Trina bawled for an entire week.

The house was perfect for us because it had two entrances one at the front and one at the back. I chose the bedroom located at the back entrance so that my neighbors could not see who was visiting me. And I always had a visitor!

∞∞∞∞

My German sugar daddy, Greg, called one night and said he really wanted to see me and was coming to visit for the weekend. My boss, Danny, was upset with me that I wanted to take the weekend off because it was a busy time of the year. He was always upset whenever I needed a break. I told him that I was taking the weekend and if he wanted to fire me he should go ahead. I was the one drawing the crowds at the club. Every weekend the place would be packed and Trina and I would make a lot of money.

Trina did not work if I was not working and I made it clear to the owner from day one because I had to ensure that no one took advantage of her. In a way I felt like I was responsible for protecting her. That made the owner even more furious to have both of his popular dancers off on the same weekend. I just didn't care. My sugar daddy needed me and I was going to make myself available for him. Greg was sending me money through Western Union all the time. He even shipped me gifts all the way from Germany, especially on special occasions like my birthday and Valentine's Day.

Greg picked me up on a Friday evening and zapped me off to an all-inclusive resort. When we walked in, the girl at the front desk checking in guests stared at me as if she recognized me. I turned my head to the side and flashed my long hair weave away from my face as I straightened my Versace sunglasses with my left hand. I made sure that the huge diamond ring I had posing on my married finger showed. She looked away and continued with the paperwork.

All weekend I had Greg panting and moaning. It seemed as if he could not get enough of me. He knew he had me hooked and he loved the sounds I would make and the way my body would tremble at each stroke. He also loved my big ass and I flipped it around in any position he wanted me to.

We rarely left the room and when we did we spent the evenings sitting out on the balcony. Greg ordered chocolate-covered strawberries and we sipped Moscato wine as we looked out at the moon shining over the sea. On Monday morning when he dropped me off at home before heading to the airport, I knew I had him in the palm of my hand!

∞∞∞

Trina seemed happy when I went over to her side of the house to let her know I was home. "What's going on? Why are you so happy?" I asked.

"I met someone and I think I like his spirit. I think I am going to get to know him," she told me.

"Really now. He must be a catch that he got you all twisted up," I said.

"He is really fine, Bubbler, and a lot of fun."

"Is it another Chinese boy?"

"Nah," she said rolling her eyes at me. "Why do you have to go there?"

"Stop being so sensitive. I am just playing with you. There is no need for you to be so tense."

Chris had hurt her feelings and any mention of his name or anything associated with him pissed Trina off.

After she relaxed, Trina told me she met one of Montego

Bay's finest rental car dealers, Rick, over the weekend and he took her out to eat. After dinner, he checked to make sure she was okay and has been calling since.

After Chris broke her heart, Trina had sworn off men. She went on several dates, but no one would seem to stick around for too long—she was not giving up any crotch. She was not interested in giving anyone a chance to get too close either. I was really happy that someone finally tickled her fancy, although I planned on investigating him just to make sure he was not a trickster trying to play around with her. Many of the business men around town were married with families and I just did not want her caught up in any mess.

The next day I went to Rick's business place posing as if I wanted a car to rent. He had a couple of guys working for him and a girl sitting around a desk in the small reception area attached to the mechanic shop where they serviced the cars. I was dressed in a polka dot black and white silk blouse and a white mini skirt with a pair of high-heeled, black pumps. I had on one of my blond wigs with my sunglasses covering my eyes.

"Good morning, I am here to see the owner," I smiled at the girl at the front desk as I flashed my ring finger.

"Is he expecting you?" she asked.

"No, I need to discuss some business with him."

"Okay let me check to see if he is available."

She disappeared through a side door. A few minutes later, a tall dark-skinned man came out to greet me. He introduced himself as Rick. I shook his hand and told him I wanted to discuss some rental business with him. He led me into an office and closed the door. He offered me a seat and then asked, "What can I do for you?"

I sat down and pretended to straighten the front of my blouse exposing my big titties. I crossed my legs as I leaned over and told him that my fiancée would be visiting soon from Germany and I was checking out his rates in advance. I explained to him that he usually picks up his cars from Avis, but he would be in Jamaica for a couple of weeks and I suggested to him that he should start supporting the local businesses.

"That's no problem," Rick said. "We can hook him up with some good rates."

Rick did not bat an eye at either my titties or my legs that showed as my skirt rode up my big ass. But by the end of our conversation, I knew everything about him. I charmed Rick so much he was telling me his entire life story. After spending more than 20 years in the United States, he was deported. He started the business when he returned to Jamaica with money he was sending back home to his mother. He said she held on to every penny he sent her and he was so surprised the day she handed him the bank account.

"I used to just live and squander money like it grew on trees. I am not about that life anymore. I told Mama that I was going to put every penny to good use and so I bought this building and started with a few cars and the business has grown and is still growing," Rick said with pride in his voice.

"Wow! A man with his head on his shoulder," I said praising him. He flashed me a broad smile and I continued to push for more information.

"You are such a sweetie. Your wife must really be head over heels with you," I pressed.

"No, I am not married. I have a couple kids back in America, that's it," he said.

"What about their Momma? You're not together anymore?" I inquired.

"No, we were done before I even got locked up."

I told him that I had a lovely girlfriend I could hook him up with, but he declined.

"Woman is not my problem. I can get any that I want. At this point in my life, I just need a good one who is willing to settle down with me."

That was all I needed to hear. I would make sure Trina was that woman.

∞∞∞∞

After Greg's weekend visit, he called every night to check on me. In fact, most nights he said he couldn't go to sleep until I helped him to "jerk off." I would sweet-talk him until I heard him huffing and puffing into the phone then I would blow him kisses, then say, "Good night sweetheart. I love you."

"I love you too," he would tell me.

∞∞∞∞

I was now living in style because of Greg. My hairdresser asked me one day if I knew anyone who wanted a condo to rent. She said one of her friends owned it, but she was leaving for Canada and didn't want to get rid of it. It was located in a beautiful high-rise building on the outskirts of the town right next to all the big-named hotels and had its own private beach. I told her I was interested and went to check it out. The condo was a bit pricey and I was not about to spend so much money on rent.

When I told Greg after he called that night he was excited. He knew exactly which building I was talking about and thought it was perfect; that way he would not have to stay in hotels when he came to visit anymore. He told me to not worry about the money–he would pay the rent.

CHAPTER
FOUR

After I left Kingston, Andre bought a house in the Portmore area and moved my mother and my young sister, Simone, there. Portmore is a large flat area of land, the majority of which is from reclaimed swamp situated not too far from the Kingston Harbor. It was developed as a residential area with many local beaches in close proximity. Andre told Momma that he did not like living in the ghetto and did not want Simone growing up there.

Andre grew up in the countryside, but went to live with an aunt in Kingston where he attended high school. After high school, he did some training courses before ending up working at the Wharf. He went to the countryside every chance he got to visit his folks.

The day they moved into the new house, Momma called me and said excitedly, "Ethel, you have to come and see the house, it is so beautiful." I was so sick and tired of telling her that I hated that name, but she still called me by it.

When I did not respond she said, "Oh, I am sorry, I

forget you said to call you Mercedes."

I promised her that I would visit during the Christmas holidays. Trina and I had not gotten a Christmas off since we started working at the club because it was the peak time of year. I decided that I was going to approach the owner, Danny, early so that he could make arrangement with the other girls.

Danny was not happy when I told him Trina and I wanted to take the last two weeks in December off and that we would be back after New Year's Day.

"You can't do me like that Bubbler. You know you are my best dancer and the holidays are when everyone comes out. No Bubbler, that's not right," he said looking as if he wanted me to feel sorry for him.

"Someone else is just going to have to do it. I need to spend the holidays with my folks," I said. I stood my ground. So during the weeks that followed, Danny didn't have much to say to me. He kept it strictly business between us!

∞∞∞∞

When the taxi pulled up at the gate, Simone was sitting on the verandah with Momma and when she saw me she jumped off the chair and ran right into my arms. I picked her up off the ground and twirled her around. Simone was growing up and she had nothing for Momma–she looked exactly like her daddy–light-skinned with curly hair and hazel eyes. I went home with a heap of stuff for her.

Momma had fixed up the house nicely. The furniture in the living room was new. Her bedroom set was new too, but she had put her old set in the other room for Simone to use.

She had good taste and everything was well-coordinated.

While the house looked lovely inside, it was hot as hell. The pre-fabricated concrete slab that the builder used kept the heat in. Even with fans in every room, I was still burning up; and by nightfall the mosquitoes came charging in. I had never seen mosquitoes so big and brazen before. They latched onto my skin when I tried to brush them away. Momma gave me some mosquito repellent and that helped some. She said that it was the swamp land near the sea that encouraged their breeding. We never had any problems like that living in our big yard. If there were mosquitoes, we would just light a fire in the back of the yard and smoke them out.

Momma introduced me to her neighbor as her "big daughter" who was in the entertainment industry and was working in Montego Bay. I did dress like a big timer in expensive clothes and nice jewelry.

"That's nice Pearl," the woman said to my mother.

She looked at me and asked, "which entertainer do you perform with?"

Before I could open my mouth to respond Momma said, "We have to run along now." She ushered me inside the house.

"She is so damn nosy," my mother said. "She always want to know everything."

When Andre came home from work and saw me he gave me a hug. "How was the drive down?" he asked.

"Not bad, the roads were clear," I told him.

"That's good. How is life treating you?"

"Everything's good. Working hard, that's just about it."

He gave Momma a peck on the cheek and went to check

on Simone who was taking a nap. I had to make sure I checked myself and that I did not show any attitude toward him in front of Momma. After all, he was no longer her lover who I thought was not going to stick around for very long. He was now my stepdaddy. She and Andre looked so happy and content together. I also realized that Momma had really changed. She was even going to church now and had her bible sitting on her night table that she read before going to bed every night.

After Momma started going to church, she told Andre she could not continue to live with him in sin and that they needed to get married. She said she didn't want any excitement and so they had a private ceremony. In fact, most of their neighbors thought that Andre and Momma were already married because of the big ass diamond ring she wore on her wedding finger.

As Momma's life improved, she began to look into ways that would help her with her progress. She applied to the United States Embassy and got a ten-year visitor's visa. She then started travelling to Miami to buy clothes and shoes to sell. At first she was just selling from her verandah and to people in the area, but Andre bought her a car and she began packing the goods in the car trunk and driving around to different office buildings after dropping Simone off at school. Momma's business quickly grew and in no time she branched out and got a booth in the Arcade in downtown Kingston. Her life had totally turned around and Simone was growing up in a good environment, unlike me. But I was very happy for her!

I had a great two weeks with my family and when it was time to leave, I was actually sad. Simone cried when the taxi came. I hugged her tightly and kissed her all over before handing her to Momma. I could hear her crying as the taxi drove down the street.

Trina and I met up downtown to take a mini-bus back to Montego Bay. She told me that her old boyfriend, Chris, came over her house to talk with her and he said that he was sorry for the way he dumped her. He claimed that he was just mad that she ran out on him. She said that he wanted to have sex with her but she told him she was not interested; she was now seeing someone else. Trina actually had a smirk on her face while she was telling me this and I wish I was there to see Chris' reaction, especially after the way he dumped her.

CHAPTER
FIVE

Business was booming at the club. It had become a hot spot for both tourists and locals. Danny, the owner, told me one day that he needed to discuss a business arrangement with me and I got a bit nervous. He had started to get really cozy with me. One night after my final act, he came into the dressing room to flirt with me in Trina's presence. When Danny walked into the room, he complimented me on doing a great act. "Bubbler, you had everyone screaming for more. You are so talented." I just smiled. Then he came over to where I was standing and resting his hand on my butt, while looking straight into my face said, you look sexy tonight."

I did not respond. He smiled and walked out of the room.

"What's gotten into him, Bubbler?" Trina asked.

"Beats me," I responded.

"He wants some of this," Trina said slapping me on the behind.

"Girl please. He will never see or smell this crotch not even if he is paying me," I laughed.

Danny had made several passes at me before and had smart remarks to say, but I had always kept him in check. I did not want to fool around with him because he was in control of my livelihood. All I was interested in was doing my job and making my money. Furthermore, I did not find him attractive enough to give him my crotch for free and he was not interested in me being his woman.

Danny was pretty much sleeping with any woman who allowed him to. He was very handsome and women would go crazy to be with him, but he did not have the light skin and curly hair that I liked. So the night he came and told me that he needed to talk with me the next day about the business, I could not sleep all night. I kept trying to figure out what the heck he needed to talk with me about. I was not scheduled to work, but he said I should meet him in his office around mid-day.

"Hey beautiful," Danny greeted me when I walked into his office at the back of the club. He was puffing on a joint and sipping on some Guinness Stout.

"Have a seat here man," he motioned to a chair across from him. He never really allowed any of his dancers in his back office. He was usually there with his boys conducting business or kicking back.

"Would you like a drink?" he asked.

"Not right now," I told him.

"Well Bubbler, I have been thinking. The club is doing great, but it is taking up a lot of my time. You are my best dancer. You know that?" I nodded my head and he continued, "But you are also very smart and seem to have your head on your shoulders. I have been watching how you conduct yourself with the customers and how skillful you are with them. I was thinking of slowing pulling you out of the dancing role and let you help me run the business. You could still dance on the weekends, if you like, but I think we could find some girls with talents to do the dancing. What do you say?"

I sat staring at him dumbfounded. All I could think of were the words "help me run the business." When I finally snapped out of my trance I said, "Me, helping you to run the business. How?"

"Well I need someone to help me manage everything: schedule the dancers and keep them in line; keep a track of the liquor and make sure everything runs smoothly with the bartenders and the bouncers; pay the bills and lock away the money at the end of the night," Danny said.

I sat there looking dazed. He trusted me to do all of this–lock away his money at night. Was he going crazy? I wondered.

Danny said that he was involved in some other business that required more of his time and so he could think of no one else who was willing to manage his club for him. He was cool with one of the bouncers, but he said the guy did not want to take on so much responsibility. The other guys had been working for him for a while, but he said that he didn't trust them enough to give them that responsibility. He wanted to start training me the following day.

When I told Trina she was shocked. "Bubbler, that don't sound right. He trusts you with all of that? Are you sure he is not trying to set you up or something?"

"Set me up! For what?" I asked.

"I don't know, but something sounds fishy to me," she said.

"Well, I am taking him up on his offer. You never know, I might own my own club someday. This might be a good experience," I told her.

"Just be careful," she warned. "You don't know what he might be involved with."

"I hear you," I said.

The next afternoon before the club opened for business, I turned up ready to start my training to be the manager. Danny gathered everyone around and said, "Listen up. Bubbler is now going to be my business manager helping me to keep a handle on things around here starting today. Everyone is going to report directly to her and if there is a problem she will let me know. I have some business dealings that are going to take me away for a few days out of the week and when I am gone she is in charge."

Except for one of the bouncers and Trina, everyone else look like they had just seen a ghost. The bouncer looked away as if he already knew what was going on and Trina had a smirk on her face. Unable to speak, the others just stood there staring at Danny and me. One of the bartenders, Bert, eventually said, "That's what's up. That's cool; that's cool with me."

I never really had any problems with Bert. In fact, he always treated me with respect and never approached me inappropriately like the bouncers and the other bartender would. They always tried to grab my behind or touch me in places that they had no business touching. When I ignored them, they tried to involve me in lewd conversations. On several occasions, I told them that they could not pay for my service because I did not entertain broke ass men.

Both the DJs were cool too and pretty much did not care

about anything other than to make sure they selected the right music and kept the crowd entertained. Trina and the new dancer, Sandra, were already my peeps so there were no concerns there. My biggest opposition was going to be the two other dancers who were at the club before Trina and I arrived. They pretty much kept out of my way, but the tension and dislike among us was so real it made the air around us feel stiff and uneasy. After Danny's speech, they looked at each other with blank stares on their faces. I looked straight at them, but they could not look directly at me.

After the first week, I realized that the work was much more than I thought it would be. Not only was I running the club, I was also acting as Danny's personal assistant dealing with customers and pacifying problems. When he gave me my first pay, I told him, "Hell no. I am going back to dancing." I made more dancing than the flat salary he was giving me. So we decided that I was going to dance on Friday and Saturday nights and only manage the business when he was out of town for two or three days during the week. Danny said he would still pay me the salary for the week.

During the weeks that followed, the two dancers started doing their own thing and would not take any direction from me and often acted like I was invisible. "Oh yeah, well I am going to put these bitches in check," I thought to myself. One day they did not show up when they were scheduled to dance and at the last minute, I had to call Trina and Sandra and ask if they would come in. I had told Danny that I was going to replace them and he told me I should try and work with them. I knew he was messing with one or probably both of them because that's how he operated, so he wanted them around. But I had enough.

"Look Danny, either you let me replace these bitches or you can find someone else to help you with your business. They don't like me, and I don't like them either. We cannot work together because they won't listen to me," I told him over the phone.

"Calm down, Bubbler; calm down," he said. "What's jumping off now?"

"They are getting under my skin, Danny, and I just can't do it anymore."

He reluctantly agreed that they should go. I personally started looking around to recruit two dancers before getting rid of them and it did not take me very long. My hairdresser told me about two girls who danced at a club in Ocho Rios and I decided to check them out one night.

Kenya had a big ass, smooth chocolate-brown skin and when she smiled her white teeth was visible in the dark. I could not take my eyes off her as she shook her ass to the beat of the music, twirled and teased the audience as the men screamed and shouted for more. I instantly saw myself in her.

Rosie was slender and was built like a model with long legs and big titties. She flashed her long Indian-looking hair over her shoulder as she danced in such a seductive way that the men were probably imagining making love to her. I thought she would be good for the after-work crowd that usually consisted of high profile, married men, looking for some excitement before going home to their wives. Kenya, on the other hand, would be perfect for the unruly weekend crowd that just wanted some excitement. These men usually have chicks all over the place and were ready to sleep with anyone, anywhere.

I waited patiently for Rosie and Kenya as they got ready

to leave the club before approaching them. I did not want to risk getting into a confrontation with the club owner. Kenya came out first and threw herself at a man waiting by the door. Unable to talk with her privately, I approached them and said, "Great act. You sure know how to please your audience." They both looked at me somewhat suspicious and then I said, "I manage a club in Mo-Bay, can I interest you into coming to work there? You could make a lot of money." I handed her my business card.

"Call me and we can talk." Without saying anything, she took the card and walked away with the dude hanging onto her impatiently.

I hung around in the club as long as I could looking for Rosie, but when I didn't see her I decided to leave. I almost didn't recognize her when she walked past me in the parking lot. She must have taken a back door to the parking lot. She seemed startled when I approached her about dancing as if she was not the person I just saw on stage. I knew those tricks all too well because whenever I was off the stage, I was a totally different person. I dressed in nice expensive garments and looked more like a business woman than a stripper. After I explained to her who I was and what my proposition was she relaxed a bit.

"I am in college," she said. "I only dance a few nights each week to make some money. I am not going to be doing this forever."

"Well I am not looking for someone who is going to be strip dancing forever. I am just giving you a chance to make some more money. I guarantee you that if you dance at the club I am in charge of, you will make twice what you make here," I said convincingly.

Rosie took my card and promised to come by the club to check it out the following night. The next day when Kenya called me I also invited her to come by and check out the scene. Danny's club was not only larger but was more popular than the one where they worked. The crowd was mixed with mostly tourists and business people and not a lot of locals except on the weekends. Before the night was over, I had both girls taking up my offer and I immediately fired the other two dancers. They were furious.

"Who the hell do you think you are? Danny must be really tripping over your big ass to give you such power. You are walking around here acting like you are better than us. You are just a whore, that's what you are—a big ole whore!" one of them shouted.

I calmly smiled and held the door open for them to leave after they collected all their things from the dressing room. There was no sense in arguing with them. I was in charge and they could not change that. I now had my crew—Trina, Sandra, Kenya and Rosie—and I was going to make things work for all of us. I was also going to make sure Danny knew that my girls were not his pawns to use whenever he felt like it. There were plenty of tricks running around in Montego Bay for him to get his kicks with. Things were going to be different going forward. Business is business and I was keeping it straight.

∞∞∞∞

Everything was running so smooth at the club, I hardly saw Danny anymore. We talked several times during the day, but he was always away conducting his other business. The club had pretty much become his second fiddle, but I did not mind because I had things under control. Everyone was working together and I felt like I had created a great team. I started to look into ways to change the image of being a "strip club" to a place of "entertainment" for everyone. I told Danny about my plans and he said I should go ahead–he was obviously involved in bigger and better things and so pretty much gave me free reign to do whatever I wanted. All he was interested in was emptying out the safe where I placed his money each night, a few times a week, and meet with me on the weekends for a few hours to go over the bills that needed to be paid and to pay his staff.

One night after I counted all the money and got ready to put it inside the safe to lock it up, I heard someone tap on the door. I looked through the glass opening and saw Bert, one of the bartenders. As I opened the door to see what he wanted, two dudes jumped from behind. One held a gun to Bert's head and the other to mine. They told Bert to lay face-down on the floor, and as one of the dudes stood guard over him the other held me by my neck, picked up the cash I had on the table and demanded that I open the safe. I refused and he gun-butted me in my head. I fell to the floor with blood streaming down my face.

"Gal, open this now or I am going to mess you up tonight," he demanded.

I sat on the floor and did not move. The dude standing over Bert then said, "Okay since she wants to play tough let's wipe him out first." He cocked the gun.

"No, please don't kill me," Bert cried.

Holding the gun to his head, the dude ignored Bert's plea.

"Bubbler, please open the safe and give them what they want," he begged me.

I did not move.

"Bubbler, please," he repeated.

At this point, I got up off the floor, walked over to the safe and tossed the money at them. I made sure I got a good look at each of their face since they did not even bother to hide it. They took the money, stuffed it inside their shirts and walked out of the room with their guns in their hands.

When I called Danny to tell him what had happened, he hit the roof. We had a great night and had made several thousand dollars in addition to what was already in the safe. He left whatever he was doing and drove to the club. Trina cleaned up my cut and wrapped my head with some bandage. Danny did not want to call the police. He said he would handle it on his own.

"I don't like cops messing in my business. They are worse than the blasted punks," he said.

"Did you get a good look at these fools, Bubbler," he asked me. I assured him I did.

"And what did you want in here?" he growled at Bert.

"Are you a part of this? Did you plan this?" he interrogated him.

Bert swore up and down that he did not know the dudes and was just as surprised as I was when they came barging into the room. He said he just wanted to tell me that he was leaving for the night. Danny gave me a gun and said that if something like this should ever happen again I should "shoot first and then ask questions."

It did not take Danny very long to get information on the punks who robbed the club. He had been operating the club for a very long time and knew pretty much everyone in the area. He was confident that they were not from out-of-town because they knew about the safe and exactly where it was kept. Someone close to him had to have given out that information. He tracked down the two dancers who I had fired, but both of them said they did not have anything to do with the robbery.

"Are you sure you are not lying?" Danny asked.

"Why would I lie. I have nothing to do with who robbed your club. Since your bitch kicked me out, I don't think about you' all," one of them told Danny.

"Yeah, I know you are upset. But let me tell you, if you are a part of this robbery, I will know."

"Listen Danny, I have nothing to do with it." She sucked her teeth then disconnected the call.

Danny laughed and said, "She thinks I am playing. Just watch what I will do."

Information quickly surfaced that two punks were seen with a lot of cash and that one offered to buy a Kawasaki bike from a man in the area. Danny knew them very well because they had delivered weed to him at the club before and they knew that he kept the safe in the back office. They thought that since he was no longer present at the club as before, they could get away with robbing it.

Danny paid some guys to bring them to him. When they brought the punks to him, he kicked the punks' asses until they told him that they would return whatever money they had remaining to him. Those two punks bawled like babies as Danny used a piece of wood to beat their asses. He told them to tell their friends that if any of them try to pull a stunt like that on him again, he was going to blow their brains to pieces.

"I am warning you, if any of you ever fuck with me like this again, I am going to kill your ass. Now get the hell out of my place and go get my money."

I saw another side of Danny that I had never seen before—tough, rugged and in control. I was so used to the lover boy or ladies' man image he displayed that this other person surprised me. Being from the ghetto, I was used to the rough kind of men and seeing Danny in this role actually sparked a curiosity in me. I wanted to get to know him more.

CHAPTER
SIX

Trina and her new friend, Rick, the rental car owner, had become a couple. She was always busy going out with him and no longer had any time to spend with me. She claimed that I was too busy running the club and taking care of Danny and that I was the one who did not have any time for her. Either way, we no longer spent any time together outside of work. Rick did not like the idea of her working at the club and so tried numerous times to get her to quit. He even offered to pay for Trina to go to cosmetology school, but she refused. She said she did not want to depend on him in case the relationship did not work out.

"Girl, you are crazy. This is something you wanted to do for so long and someone's offering to pay for it; you better take him up on his offer," I encouraged her.

When she did not respond I continued, "Look at it this way Trina, if the relationship does not work out and you have to come back to work at the club to finish school so be it, but get what you can while he is willing to give it. Yeah, you are making him grin so it's okay if he wants to spend some money on you."

Trina had been trying so hard to save up money to go to school, but every time she had enough money and decided it was time, something happened back home in Kingston that she had to take care of. Rick was her way out and I encouraged her to run with his offer.

∞∞∞∞

The incident at the club seemed to have brought Danny and me closer. He was always checking up on me to make sure that I was okay even when I was not at work. He said that he did not want anyone to retaliate against me for the beatings he laid down on the two punks. I got so comfortable with him that one night after we closed the club and everyone left, I decided to kick back with him for a while in the back office. I sat on the large leather sofa he had against the wall, and we started out innocently sipping on some Moscato wine.

"You know Bubbler, I thought you were a real bitch when you started working here," Danny looked at me and said jokingly.

He continued, "I only tolerated your ass because you were bringing the crowd to the club and helping me make money. I don't know what it was but something just told me that I could trust you to run the business for me. I am really glad I took a chance on you."

"And I thought you were an asshole too, wanting to sleep with every woman who crosses your path. I don't give out my crotch to just anyone without getting something in return," I told him.

He laughed, got up off the chair and knelt down in front of me. "Do you still feel that way? Do you think all I want is to get into your panties?" he asked.

A chill went through my body and it was instantly covered in goose bumps. For the first time since meeting Danny, I looked straight at his face and saw a pair of light brown eyes full of life and vigor looking straight back at me. He cupped my face in his hands and softly whispered, "Bubbler, you are a beautiful soul."

Before I could resist he was kissing me so passionately that all I could do was kiss him back. He began to rub his hand up my leg as the mini-dress I was wearing slowly inched its way further up. I shifted my ass to each side so that he could pull the dress over it and then he lifted it over my head. I began to unbutton his shirt. He stood up and backed the shirt off and dropped his pants and underwear in a pile on the ground. His more than 200-pound body was firm with his muscles bulging and no flabs anywhere. I instantly got excited. I was reminded of the 32-year-old lover I had back in Kingston banging me.

Back then, I was a vivacious 21-year-old young woman with an insatiable appetite for sex. I moved from one dude to another looking for more and more pleasure. Then I found exactly what I was looking for–a 32-year-old dude who lived with his baby's mother. The first time he jacked me up, I thought I was in heaven. I screamed so loud I knew the people in the room next door in the cheap motel must have heard me. After that first time every chance he got my old dude would snatch me up and whisk me off somewhere where we could be together. I was so loving it that I never objected to going anywhere with him until one day his baby's mother saw me in his car and threatened to beat my ass. I quit hanging with him then.

∞∞∞∞

I snapped out of my thoughts as Danny had his hands all over my body. I pulled a condom from the stock I kept in my purse and handed it to him. He looked at me, smiled and without saying a word took the wrapper off and put the condom in place. He turned me around and all I felt was pleasure as my body released all the tension it had built up over the last several weeks as Danny gasped for air.

"God dammit, Bubbler. Damn woman, you have been keeping this from me for so long," he said.

I just looked at him and smiled. I was so busy running the club for the last several weeks that I had not been involved in any sexual activities with anyone. I was making enough money now, plus Greg was sending money every month so I was not desperate where I had to entertain men for money anymore.

When I got home, I noticed that Greg had called several times. I was not in the mood for any sex talk that night so I turned the ringer off on the phone and bundled up in bed.

∞∞∞∞

After Trina started cosmetology school, Rick started pressuring her into moving in with him. He said that it would save her the money she was paying in rent. He also convinced her to work at his business on the weekends instead of going to the club so that she could still have money to help out her family. She agreed so I didn't see much of her anymore. I tried to call Trina every day to make sure that she was okay and Rick was not taking advantage of her. Rick's mother had taken to Trina and kept asking him when they were getting married.

"You need to do the right thing. It doesn't look good shacking up with her like that. Trina deserves better," Rick's mother told him.

He laughed and said, "Mama, we will get married soon."

"Soon? When will that be? Aren't both of you together long enough? What are you waiting for?"

"We are not trying to rush it."

"If she is good enough to live with, then she is good enough to be your wife. Rick, you need to hurry up and marry that girl."

On her 25th birthday, Rick threw a huge surprise party for Trina and invited all her friends and family. A bus load of people came from Kingston. He said she was now a quarter century old and so he wanted to make this birthday special. He rented the club and I was excited to be involved with the arrangements. Rick took her shopping and brought her a sexy black dress for the occasion. He told her he was taking her out to the club to spend the evening.

When Rick and Trina arrived at the club and everyone shouted, "happy birthday Trina," she burst into tears. Almost everyone including her mother, sister and brothers came to Montego Bay for the party. After she cut her birthday cake and Rick opened a bottle of champagne, he went down on his knee, pulled out a ring from his pocket and proposed to her. This time everyone cried.

∞∞∞∞

Danny called me one morning at home to ask if I wanted to go on a mission with him. "A mission," I repeated. "That sounds like some church business. I ain't got no time for that right now."

He laughed and I could just see those big white teeth surrounded by his big ass lips. I closed my eyes for a minute as I remembered him playfully holding my nipples between his teeth as if he was going to bite them. He was totally not attractive to me, but heck he knew how to get me aroused and touch me in places where I wanted to be touched and that was all I needed until Greg decided to jump on a plane to service his "Nubian Princess" as he called me. I was not looking for a lover man. I just wanted a good cock every now and again.

"Are you still there?" Danny asked as I drifted off into my imagination.

"Yeah, where did you say you wanted me to go with you?" I asked.

"I am heading to the countryside–St. Elizabeth, and I wanted to see if you would go with me. I would love to have your company."

"Countryside," I repeated. "Why? I don't like bushes and ticks and all that mess. You know I only go to places where there are street lights, paved roads and piped water?"

"They have all of that there Bubbler, just come with me, you'll see."

I reluctantly told him I would.

"Oh, throw on a pair of jeans and some comfortable shoes; we might do a bit of walking. I want to show you something."

When Danny came to pick me up he was dressed in jeans, a polo shirt and a pair of Timberland boots. He had on a pair of Prada sunglasses and a baseball cap and he was driving a Range Rover instead of his Lexus. Danny always dressed like a business man and this was the first time I was seeing him in casual wear and I was really digging the look. I instantly felt hot all over. He looked like such a rough hoodlum who I wanted to sleep with on the spot.

"Nice place," he said motioning to my condominium building. "You are living in style."

"Yeah," I said as if it was not a big deal.

"I hope I get a chance to see the inside soon."

I did not respond. I had decided from day one that the only man allowed in my condo was Greg. That place was off limits to everyone else no matter how good they were in bed.

We headed out of Montego Bay on our journey to St. Elizabeth. I had passed through there only once before on a beach trip to Negril and quite frankly did not even remember what it looked like. I only knew that we passed through a lot of bushes and trees with houses perched on the hillsides. I think we also passed through the town of Santa Cruz, which did not seem like much to me at the time.

Danny put a CD with lyrics coming from Beres Hammond, a Jamaican reggae entertainer, in the player and I chilled back in my seat enjoying the music. The song, "*She loves me now*," started playing and Danny started singing over Beres' voice. I looked at him, laughed and said, "You are so stupid. Don't confuse sex with love."

Along the way, I learned that Danny was actually from St. Elizabeth and not Montego Bay. He left home to work in Montego Bay after high school, but all his family was still in

St. Elizabeth. I would not have imagined that he was a
country boy. He was slick and cunning and operated like he
was a big city boy. The first time Trina and I met him in New
Kingston, I actually thought that was where he was from but
was just doing business in Montego Bay.

∞∞∞∞

After driving for about two hours, we finally got to
Danny parents' house. They had a beautiful four bedroom
concrete house on several acres of land. His mother was a
petite Chinese woman with slanted eyes and a very soft voice
while his father was tall and dark and walked with a limp.
Danny said that he used to work with the Bauxite Industry as
a crane operator and had a terrible accident that almost took
his life. After the company settled with him, he built the
house and went into farming and he never worked for anyone
again.

Danny's dad was into me, asking all kinds of questions,
but his mom sat quietly observing me. I could feel her eyes
staring at me and I didn't think she was feeling me. She
offered us some food she had made earlier. It was the best
ackee and saltfish with boiled dumplings and yellow yam I
had in a long while. It was so good, not even my
grandmother's cooking came anywhere near hers. His mother
looked happy that I was enjoying her food and I think that
made her warm up to me a little.

Danny picked some coconuts from a tree at the side of
the house and we sat on the verandah drinking the juice and
talking. After a couple of hours, he told his parents that we
were heading out.

"You're not going to wait until Thelma comes home?" his father asked. Thelma was Danny's younger sister who had moved back home with her two children after divorcing her husband. She was at work and the children were in school.

"Nah, I got some business to take care of. I am just passing through," Danny said. "But I will see you all on Sunday. Mama cook some curry goat for me nuh?"

"Yes, yes, I will do that." She smiled and nodded her head.

I could tell that she enjoyed cooking and feeding him. When we drove off, I playfully said, "You better make sure that you find a woman like your mother or you are going to be eating at restaurants every day."

"I can help myself. I can cook anything I want to eat," he said. "No woman has to worry about me that's why I live alone. Women come with too much drama and stress."

"Really now. So why do you still bother with them?"

"We can't live with them and we can't live without them," he said as he laughed and winked at me.

The schools had been dismissed and Danny pulled alongside the road and asked a young boy if he had seen Damion.

"Yes, he just went back inside to get a book," the boy responded. The boy kept on walking down the road. So young and innocent, I thought.

A few minutes later a boy around nine or ten came through the school gate dragging a school bag that was too big for him to carry. The boy looked just like Danny. When he saw the Range Rover, he ran toward it shouting, "Daddy, oh Daddy."

Danny hopped out and took the bag from the boy and

hugged him. Then he introduced me to the boy as "Miss Mercedes." I had never heard him call me by that name before and it actually sounded sexy on his lips. He had introduced me to his parents as Ms. Ford, his business manager. When he took the boy home, the boy's Momma came running out the house to see who Danny had in the vehicle with him. When she saw me she started cursing, "I told you before I don't want any of your women around my child. Furthermore, why are you bringing your whore here? I don't want to see her."

"Relax, man, relax. Why you always trying to embarrass yourself in front of people. Just relax. She is not my whore; she is my manager. She is managing the club. Furthermore, he is my son too so you can't dictate what I do when he is in my presence."

"Danny, please. You sleep with every woman who crosses your path. You act like you have the best cock in the whole wide world," she said.

"You should know. Probably that's why you stay mad with me. I guess you miss it," he said teasingly.

"I was a damn fool. Young and fool, fool that's what I was. I should have been studying my books instead of studying you." She sucked her teeth and walked back toward the house. She was a skinny woman with long legs. She was wearing a pair of cutoffs showing her butt cheeks and a spaghetti strap blouse with no bra.

Danny laughed. Shaking his head he got into the vehicle and drove off. Half a mile down the road he was still laughing. I sat beside him thinking that I didn't know he had a son. Actually, I didn't know much about him although I had been working with him for so long.

We drove for about half an hour in silence and then Danny turned the vehicle off the main road unto a dirt road. The Range Rover bounced up and down as he tried to avoid the vehicle going into the large potholes along the dirt road.

"Where are you taking me?" I asked. All I saw around us were thick clumps of bushes on both sides of the road and some long ass trees stretching for miles in the distance.

"I told you I don't do bush, 'cause I don't like ticks," I said.

He did not respond; he just kept on driving. We got to the foot of a hill and he said we had to get out and walk.

"Walk to where? Are you damn crazy or what?" I asked.

"That's why I told you to wear comfortable shoes. Come on and stop complaining."

He held my hands and I kept close to him as we walked along a beaten track. We went over a hill and then I almost fainted because of what I saw before us. There was a large field of marijuana with lush green leaves blowing to the slight wind passing through the trees as the late afternoon sun bore down on us. Just looking at so much weed in one place, I instantly felt an irie feeling came over me.

"This is my other business that is keeping me busy," he said.

"What the hell, Danny! Who is taking care of all of this for you?"

"I have some guys who come early in the morning to water them and make sure everything is okay. We just harvested along that side–he pointed to an area which was bare–and this side will be ready in a few weeks. I have two other plots further down near the river that we just planted."

"You're not scared of the police and soldiers?" I asked.

"No, not really. The only way they can find this is if they are using one of the small search planes. They won't take the chance because of the hill, it's dangerous for the plane." He sounded confident as if he knew what he was saying. I picked a couple branches off one of the trees to take home to make tea. Growing up, my grandmother used to boil marijuana tea all the time. She said it was good for her system.

Later that evening when Danny took me to my condo, he got out of the vehicle, pulled me close to him and kissed me so tenderly, one would think that I was his woman. He held me for a while as he stared into my eyes and said, "You are so beautiful. Thank you so much for spending the day with me. Don't bother about coming to the club tonight, I will handle things. Get some rest and I will talk with you tomorrow."

I gave him a peck on his cheek and walked toward the main entrance of my building swinging my ass from side-to-side. I could feel his eyes staring at my behind. When I got inside my condo, I instantly called Trina.

"Is Rick nearby?" I asked. I always had to check to make sure he was not around. I was not comfortable having a conversation with her if he was in her presence.

"No, he is still at the business," she said.

"Good, good," and I went into telling her about my field trip with Danny.

"What? He took you to see his parents, and then he picked up his son and took him home knowing that his Momma was home, then he showed you his weed field and then he kissed you like you are his woman," she repeated everything I told her.

"Yes, my dear."

"Bubbler, I don't know but it sound like he has fallen for you. How many times did you slept with him? Only once and already he is acting like a love-sick puppy? Girl, you must have some real good crotch."

We both laughed.

"I don't like him like that Trina, I really don't. He is cool and all, but he is not attractive to me. You know I like light-skinned dudes with curly hair."

"That's why you are so wrapped up with that German dude. No wonder when he visits you act like you're all in love. Greg this, Greg that," she sounded retarded.

"I don't sound like that," I laughed. "Greg is White, not light-skinned."

"Same thing; they all have pale looking skin. I don't care about all that I just need a good man to treat me right. I will take Chinese, Indian or Negro as long as he treats me right."

"Don't I know," I said as her old Chinese boyfriend, Chris, crossed my mind.

"Rick is perfect for me. I love his Black ass so I don't need anyone else. You need to stop worrying about skin color and just find you a good man. What do you even know about Mr. German anyway? Just that whenever he can, he jets out here to get some of your big ass!"

After I hung up the phone, Trina had me really thinking. I knew nothing about Greg. He had never talked about his family or what he did for work. When we started getting close and he asked me what kind of work I did in addition to entertaining men and I told him that I was an event planner for entertainers. Although at the time I was just a dancer, but to some extent managing the club had put me in that event planning role. I decided that the next time Greg visited I was going to find out about him and what he really wanted from me.

CHAPTER
SEVEN

I rolled into Kingston with Danny on a Friday morning to make a drop downtown. He was regularly supplying weed to a guy who owned a restaurant who was then parceling it out and selling it pound-by-pound to other dudes. They were in turn rolling it and selling it as joints. Danny was the head of the game—farming, and selling in bulk. I asked him why he didn't build his own team to do the distribution and he said he had no time to deal with any crazy, small time dudes. According to him, it was too much work trying to keep track of the distributors even though he would make more money. It was also too risky because if they go down they usually bring down the boss with them. He preferred to deal with one person; he dropped off the load, collected his money and kept it moving.

After we did the drop, Danny took me shopping and I bought a couple outfits and shoes to match for Reggae Sunsplash. Greg had hinted that he might be coming, but then he said he could not because he had things to take care of back in Germany. When Danny mentioned taking me to Reggae Sunsplash, I hesitated at first. If Greg was coming, my first priority would have been to make sure I spent time with him. I had to make sure my rent money kept coming each month.

"Really Danny. You want to take me to Reggae Sunsplash?"

"Yeah, I would love to have you there with me; if you are available."

Smiling I held onto his hand as I rubbed his palm and said, "Of course I am available. I would love to go with you."

"You are going to have a good time – I promise." He winked at me and walked away.

∞∞∞∞

After we were through shopping, I called my mother to tell her I was in town and she said she was by my grandmother's house in our old neighborhood. When the Lexus slowly rolled up on our narrow, dusty zinc-lined street, everyone we passed cocked their head trying to see who was driving. One of my older boy cousins and some friends sat on the wall in front of my grandmother's house smoking and chilling when we pulled up.

"Rass Bubbler, I didn't even realize that's you," he said to me when I got out of the car to give him a hug.

"Give me a money nuh?" he begged. I pushed my hand in my pocket and pulled out some bills and handed them to him.

"Respect my cousin, respect! You look good though. Is that your man?" he asked pushing up his mouth to indicate he was referring to Danny.

I turned my head sideways and whispered to him, "My main squeeze for now."

"You know how we do it," I said playfully.

"You and your mother are something else. But she is changed now. She is around the back of the yard with Mama."

I told Danny to pull the car up on the curbside and follow me. We walked up on Momma, Grandma and my aunt, Crystal, as they sat on a bench under the mango tree chatting. From the expression on each of their faces, I just knew they were murdering someone with their mouths. Grandma was the first one to turn her head around and when she saw us she squeaked, "My Lord, Ethel. You are about to give me a heart attack. Come over here and give the old lady a hug chile."

"What did you bring for me?" she asked. Without waiting for me to answer she continued, "And who is this nice gentleman you have here with you?"

I introduced Danny as the owner of the club that I worked at.

"So you are the one having her shaking her behind in front of everyone?" my grandmother asked.

Danny laughed, shook his head and said, "She is not dancing anymore. She is the club manager making sure everything runs smoothly."

"The manager. You are not dancing anymore?" my aunt asked. Turning to my mother she said, "Pearl, I thought you said she was in Montego Bay as a dancer."

Before they could prolong the conversation I cut them off, "So what are you all up to now?"

"Nothing, just chilling," Momma answered.

"You're not at the Arcade today? And where's Simone?" I asked. I longed to hold my sister and nibble on her soft fat cheeks.

"No, business kind of slow now so I am taking a break today. I have some barrels coming tomorrow, in time for the Independence holiday next week. It's going to be very busy so I am on slow motion this week," Momma said.

She pushed her head through the back door and hollered, "Debbie, bring Simone come, Ethel is here."

Danny looked at me with a bewildered look on his face as if to say, "Who is Ethel?" I ignored him and pushed passed Momma to go through the door to get Simone myself. When she saw me, Simone jumped up from off the sofa where she was sitting down, while she watched TV, and ran to me. I picked her up, twirled her around and covered her face with wet kisses. She laughed and kicked and laughed some more. I took her outside to meet Danny. My aunt got up off the bench to make space for Danny to sit. She then sat on an old pail turned upside down. I squeezed in on the bench between him and Momma with Simone in my arms. He played around with her for a few minutes and then reminded me about the bag I had in the trunk of the car. He offered to get it for me. As usual, I had plenty of stuff for Simone: clothes, toys and children movies.

I had a bag of clothes that I was no longer wearing that I took with me to give Momma for anyone who needed them. Grandma, Aunty and Momma rumbled through the bag.

"These are too sexy for me. These are young people's style," my grandmother said as she handed a few garments she had in her hand to my aunt. Danny and I sat around and chatted with them for a while longer and then I told them that we were hitting the road. Before I left, I handed each of them some money I had with me.

"So when next am I going to see you, Ethel?" my grandmother asked.

"I will make sure to stop by the next time I am in town."

"So when will that be?"

"I don't know Grandma. I only come into town when I have things to take care of. You know it's a long drive."

"Alright take care of yourself, and give the old lady a call every now and again. Don't wait until I'm dead to miss me."

I laughed, gave her a big hug, "Grandma, you know I love you and I always miss you. Stop talking about death because you are not going to die anytime soon."

Momma walked us to the gate and as usual Simone refused to let go of me. I kissed her all over again and told her I was going down the street, I would be back. I said goodbye to my cousin and his friends sitting on the wall and we drove out to head back to Montego Bay.

"Ethel," Danny laughed. "What kind of name is that? Did your grandmother give you that old woman name or is it your pet name?"

"Actually she did. It's my real name and I hated it."

"Okay, so where did Mercedes come from?"

"That's the name I gave myself–Mercedes Ford," I said proudly.

"So, you changed your name?"

"I don't have any official papers, but that's the name I use," I said.

I explained to him that I didn't have a birth certificate and wasn't sure if my mother had registered me.

"What kind of confusion is that?" Danny said. "Okay, my sister works with the Registration Department so I am going to talk with her to see if she can help you get a birth certificate. You might have to get your school records or any information you can to verify who you are."

"I don't want a birth certificate in that name," I told him.

"Let's start first with the name you went to school with and then deal with the name change after," he said.

I used my hand to cover Danny's hand as it rested on the gear stick. He looked over at me, smiled and then back at the road. I started rubbing his palm and then moved my hand to his leg and rubbed his inner thigh. I felt so comfortable and at peace around Danny, I might eventually get to like him. He also knows how to get me hot and twisted up inside, I thought to myself. As if reading my thoughts, he pulled the car off the main road and onto a dirt road.

Danny parked the car alongside a cluster of bushes, pushed his seat backward and lowered the back. I didn't wait for him to make the first move. I sat on his lap and started kissing him. Occasionally, we saw light coming from cars passing along the main road as we explored each other's body. This created such an adrenaline rush and at the same time anxiety for us as our hearts pounded against each other. It did not take long before both of our bodies started trembling. Danny held onto me, laughed and said, "God dammit woman. I swear, you are so crazy." I kissed his lips and did not want to get off of him.

CHAPTER EIGHT

When Trina, Rick, Danny and I stepped through the gate at Reggae Sunsplash, my heart began to thump. Reggae music, the smell of weed and alcohol always messed with my brain and put me in a horny mood. I decided that I was only going to sip on a Heineken Beer because I didn't want to start acting stupid because I could not hold my liquor. We hung around rocking to the music and sipping on our bottles.

The crowd was thick and I looked around at all the bitches, looking like they came to the show to lock down a man. You could tell that they were from the ghetto because of how they dressed and acted. They were wearing all kinds of crazy looking hair weaves and see-through clothes. Although I grew up in one of the worst ghetto areas of Kingston, I dressed with a lot of class. You would never catch my Momma with all parts of her body hanging out during her trickster days. I adopted her classy way of dressing, but I loved to wear tight-fitting garments that accentuated my big ass.

We found a spot and I stood in front of Danny and he looped his arms around me with his cock resting directly on my butt. He slowly moved his hips to the beat of the music while I rocked along with him. He started to playfully nibble along my neckline. I looked over at Trina and Rick and they were locked tight facing each other as they danced. Danny placed his hand along my spine and rubbed it as he continued to nibble all over my neck while at the same time rocking to the music. He smelled so good, I wasn't sure if it was his cologne or aftershave, but he was turning me on. I felt my crotch starting to get wet. I bent his head and whispered in his ears, "If you keep this up you going to have to find some place to take care of me soon."

He laughed and said, "Okay I will behave for now."

We continued to rock from side-to-side as the crowd cheered and chanted as each artist stepped on stage to perform their act. Then my favorite artist, Pinchers, stepped on stage. He grabbed the microphone and started singing. His lyrics was all I needed to hear to 'bruk' out. Danny's slow whine could not hold me any longer. Trina joined me and both of us put on an act. It reminded me of old times by the rum bar on our street growing up. I knew Danny was an excellent dancer–hell he owned a strip club, but I had no idea Rick could move his body the way he did that night. I was so surprised. We had a good time dancing and bonding together as friends.

By the time we left the show and I got into Danny's Lexus, I was in so much heat I could hardly wait for us to get to a bed. Danny pulled into a motel about a mile from where we were. As soon as we entered the room, we were all over each other: kissing, sucking and rubbing. I climbed on top of him and took charge. In no time my scream intermixed with the creaking of the bed as I collapsed on his chest. Danny flipped me around and worked his magic. Before long he let out a long sigh. He dropped on the bed beside me and said, "Damn Bubbler, you are going to give me a heart attack."

I slowly stroked his eyebrows with my finger and said, "You are going to give me jaundice."

Danny got up off the bed and looked around, "This place is nasty. Let's get the hell out of here." We saw two large cockroaches running on the wall facing the bed.

When Danny took me home I could see that he wanted to come inside my condo, but I could not bring him into my space. We sat in the car for a few minutes chilling and just rubbing up onto each other. As much as I wanted to feel his hard body next to mine in my bed, I just had to deny myself. He did not push the issue, but gave me a kiss on my forehead as I got ready to step out of the car.

That night I wrapped myself up in my sheets and wondered, *"Why was I playing with fire?"* I knew getting involved with Danny would only create problems. My heart was not with Danny, but I could not resist him. I decided that I needed to talk with him to see what his intentions were. I thought that I probably needed to let him know straight up that I was not interested in having a relationship with him. All night, I rehearsed what I was going to say to Danny when I see him at the club the next day.

When Danny walked up behind me as I entered the door to the office and drew me close to him, I melted. All the lines I had rehearsed the night before went flying out my head. I turned around and started kissing him. I then slowly backed away, wiped my red lipstick off his lips and said, "I've got

work to do, Mr." I smiled, twirled my ass and sat down on
the chair behind the desk to go through the stack of paper I
had sitting there.

.

CHAPTER
NINE

Greg called to say that he managed to get some free time from work and booked his ticket to Jamaica for a week. I badly wanted to see him, but found myself worrying about what I was going to tell Danny in order to get the week away from work. We had gotten so close over the last few months that every move Danny made I knew about it. He had also started giving me a cut out of the money he made each time I accompanied him to Kingston to do his drop offs. He looked forward to me going with him so that he had someone to talk to on the ride. I also served as a distraction to police on the road.

On one of our trips, we ran into a police check point. By the time we realized what was going on, it was too late to turn back. The officer stepped out into the street and signaled for us to pull over to the side. I could see the nervousness in Danny's eyes when he looked over at me. He had a hundred pounds of nicely cured weed in a bag inside the trunk. I placed my hand on his and said, "Relax. Let me do the talking. I know how to handle this."

The officer stepped up to the window, "Good day guys. Can you please step out of the car? We would like to do a check?"

"Oh sure officer. What is going on? Are you searching for something or someone in particular?" I asked as I opened the door and stepped out ready to work my magic with my voice.

When he turned to answer me, our eyes met and I realized that it was Trevor, one of my mother's old sugar daddies. He was one of the nice ones who always made small talk with me and gave me ice-cream money.

"Ethel," he said. "Oh my Lord, you have grown into a really nice young woman. How is your mother doing?"

"She is doing very good, has a baby and all."

"That's good, that's so good to hear."

"Yes, I am actually on my way to visit her now."

"Oh so you don't live in Kingston anymore?"

"No, I have been in Montego Bay for the last several years. This is my fiancé, Danny," I said nudging Danny closer.

He shook Danny's hand, "Please take good care of her."

"I am not going to hold you up any longer. Tell your mother 'Hi' for me. Here's my card, if you ever run into problems with any of my officers, please call me," he remarked.

It had Trevor Mattes, Inspector of Police, written on it. I thanked him and told him I would. We got back into the car and Danny drove away.

"Thank you so much Bubbler. If I was alone I would be gone to the big house."

"How much longer are you planning on doing this?" I asked. He did not respond and I continued, "You need to quit."

"I will. I just need to set myself up right," he said.

I thought about what lies I was going to tell Danny so that I could be free when Greg arrived. I came up with a plan that I would have to seduce him first and then when I was through I would stand in front of him butt naked and tell him I need to spend a week in Kingston. My mother is going to Miami and needs me to watch Simone. It sounded good at first, but by the next day it did not make much sense. Momma always went away to Miami and different cities to buy goods to sell. Her husband always took care of Simone or she left her with my grandmother.

That night just as we closed, Danny came by the club. He went to talk with one of the bouncers, but I interrupted their conversation and pulled him aside, "I really need to talk with you." He looked a bit concerned.

"Is everything alright?" he asked.

"Babe, I need some time off from work. I need to go away somewhere quiet where I can think."

"Is the work here too much for you?" he asked.

"It's not the work. I just need a break by myself."

"Where are you planning on going?"

"Negril," I said. I did not even think about it; it came right out my mouth.

"Okay, that's fine. I will handle things while you are gone."

"Can you cancel any run you need to make in Kingston? I don't want you going by yourself."

"Are you worried that I am going to pick up some

women there? I am over that kind of life Bubbler. I told you I just need to make some money to set myself up the right way."

"I am not worried about women. I know I have you hooked on this," I said and patted my crotch.

"I am just worried about those police boys. You know that they have been stringing out on the road lately," I reminded him.

He shook his head, laughed and hugged me tightly. "I won't, I promise."

The fire was getting hotter, but I could not stop pushing the wood in. I wanted Danny, but I also wanted to see Greg. I knew that Danny was not only falling for me, but had come to depend on me for many things: I kept everything at the club in order—my team worked well together and the club continued to make money; I was escorting him to Kingston and to St. Elizabeth when he needed me to; and, I was giving him all the sex he wanted.

∞∞∞

Seeing Greg made my heart skip a beat. The first couple of days we never left the condo and barely got out of the bed. We then spent the remainder of the time at a beach house in Negril lying out in the sun as we chilled on the beach. My cell phone could not pick up any signal from where we were staying and it was a relief. I did not want to risk having Danny call me as I might have been tempted to talk with him. I finally mustered up the courage to ask Greg about himself. I played with the hairs on his chest as we laid butt naked on the bed.

"Greg, do you realize that I don't know anything about you?"

"What do you want to know about me?"

"Well you might not know my family, but I tell you everything about them. You have never talked about your family or even the work you do in Germany. I know nothing about you. Am I just your whore who you can get away to spend time with? What do you see me as Greg? What do you want from me?"

He was quiet for a while. Then he softly pinched my cheek. "Mercedes, you are very special to me. From the first day I met you I cannot seem to get you out of my mind. No, you are not my whore. I actually don't even know what I want right now, because I am scared. I love being around you. You make me feel happy, I love your body, your smile, and damn I love everything about you. I care deeply about you too and actually worry that someday you are going to break my heart. I love you, Mercedes," he said as he kissed me so passionately I felt my breath stop for a second.

"Well what about your family?" I asked.

"There's not much of a family. My parents live in the United States. My father is ex-military and spent 16 years in Germany. My brother, Courtney, and I were born there. When my father retired he returned to the United States and that's where my brother and I finished high school. I returned to Germany for college and stayed. I am divorced after a three-year stint of marriage. I have no children."

"Don't you miss your parents?"

"I do, but there is nothing I can do right now about it. I visit them as often as I can."

"Do you think you will ever leave Germany?"

He laughed when I said that and his laughter melted my heart. He was so handsome; he literally took my breath away.

"Why are you laughing?"

"It's funny you ask that because at one time I was planning on buying a house and moving here."

"Really! To Jamaica? Why?"

"I have travelled to many countries and this is the only place that makes me feel stress-free and happy. When you met me, my divorce was just finalized and I was here for those three weeks reflecting on my life and my future. I came here thinking that I was just going to spend some money on pussy, weed and liquor; have a good time and then leave. But you showed me something else—you might not realize it, but what you showed me was that you cared."

I was quiet. I did not know what to say.

"Why did you offer to sell me your body? Was that something you were doing all the time?"

"To be honest with you, I did it just for the money. I left Kingston with nothing and all I ever saw growing up was my mother entertaining different men for money. She is changed now. Since my step-daddy came into her life he has been the only man for her. But she had a hard life growing up and that's what she resorted to and I followed right in her footsteps."

"Are you still doing it?"

"No, there is no need to. You pay my rent each month and I make good money managing the club and promoting events there." My mind instantly flashed on Danny. Oh God, I thought, here I am with Greg who I could not wait to be with, but yet I am still thinking about Danny.

"Are you okay?" Greg asked. He seemed to sense that I

had something on my mind.

"Yes, I am fine. So what kind of work do you do?" I asked. I was trying to shift the conversation back to him.

"I work with an American-based company as an engineer. I travel to the U.S. several times during the year so I get to see my parents pretty often. I am thinking that someday I might return to live there. They are getting older now and although I see them often, it's not the same as living in the same country."

"What about your brother? Does he live nearby or visit them often?"

"My parents live in Washington, DC and my brother lives in California. My mother doesn't really like his lifestyle so they don't get along."

When Greg saw the puzzled look on my face he immediately said, "He is gay."

"Oh!" was all I could say.

When Greg dropped me off at the condo on his way to the airport, I was so sad. I sat on the balcony and looked out at the sea. My neighbors were also on their balcony chilling with music playing. The song, *"Torn between two lovers"* was playing on their stereo. I went back inside, threw myself across the bed and cried until I could cry no more. After I regained my composure, I picked up the phone to call Danny. I could hear the excitement in his voice when I told him I had returned home and would come to the club later in the evening.

Danny hugged me tightly and kissed my forehead when I walked into the club. Those days he did not care who was around. Actually, by then everyone knew we were together. We could not hide it even if we wanted to. I didn't know whether he believed me when I told him that I was actually taking a break by myself, but if he had any suspicion, he did not show it. He just welcomed me back with open arms.

CHAPTER
TEN

Trina's wedding was the most beautiful wedding I had
seen. Actually, it was the only wedding I had ever attended. I
was her maid-of-honor and her bridesmaids were her sister
Carol; our friend Sandra, who also worked at the club and
who she shared the house with after I moved into the condo;
and, one of her cousins who I was meeting for the first time.
The best man and all the groomsmen were Rick's friends and
family members.

They had the wedding ceremony at the church Rick's
mother attended in Ocho Rios and the reception was held at
a villa overlooking the sea not too far from the church. Rick
had a large extended family and many people he conducted
business with, as well as his friends, made up majority of
those in attendance.

The wedding gown Trina wore was beautiful with a long
train tapering from the top of her waist billowing over her ass
all the way behind her. The top portion of the dress was
covered with tiny beads while the bottom portion was

covered in lace. Her shoes were made of tiny white beads stitched together.

During the wedding ceremony, Trina's mother kept wiping away tears from her eyes. She was such a beautiful bride and her mother was, no doubt, very proud of her. Because I was in the wedding party, I could not get to be with Danny, but my eyes stalked his every move. I noticed two girls eyeing him and they were doing everything to get his attention: dropping their program that he picked up and returned; trying to talk with him while he tried to follow what was going on; and, smiling up into his face. After the ceremony and we marched out of the church, the first thing I did was to seek Danny out. Sure enough the girls were up into his face talking and laughing. I walked right up to them, threw my arms around him and said, "Babe, are you okay?" The girls quickly walked away.

During the reception, Danny sat at the table with my mother, stepfather, sister and my aunts and grandmother. I made sure that he was with my whole clan. I did not want to have to collar up anyone.

We had a wonderful time, dancing, talking and laughing. My mother and stepfather left early because they had to take my grandmother and Simone home. We stayed until the DJ turned the music off and got ready to shut everything down.

On the way to Montego Bay, Danny started telling me that he really wanted to be with me. "I love you so much, babe. I really love you." I guess the wedding ceremony must have gotten to his head.

"I think we need to get married and settle down."

"Danny, let's just take it one day at a time. You have a lot of things you want to get done and I am still trying to pull my life together. We have plenty of time to think about that."

"I understand, but I don't want us to waste too much time."

"We are not wasting time–we are enjoying each other."

He nodded his head and focused his attention on the road.

I loved Danny too, but I also loved Greg. *"Lord, please help me,"* I silently prayed.

"How am I going to get out of this situation? Do I even want to get out?" I sometimes asked myself. I was so in love with both men that when I was with one, I still wanted to see the other.

"Are you okay, Mercedes?" he asked. "You are so quiet."

"I am just tired," I said.

He had stopped calling me Bubbler and said that I was not in the club strip dancing any more so I should let go of that name. He jokingly said that the only place he wanted me to dance was in bed. He was having me more around his parents and his son too and did not think that Bubbler was appropriate. I didn't care one way or the other.

Danny headed in the direction of where the condo was located, and then I realized that I did not tell him that I had bought a house and was no longer living in the condo. Some new houses were built in Montego Bay and Trina encouraged me to buy one. The money I accumulated from escorting Danny to Kingston was used as the down payment. Trina and Rick had bought in the first phase of construction and I ended up in the third phase. I bought the house in my mother's name just in case something should happen to me, Momma would not have any problem with ownership.

"You moved and didn't tell me?"

"Danny, you have never been inside my place so what

difference would it make if I had told you?"

"You are right, I was never invited in."

"Oh it's not that serious—there wasn't nothing much about it anyway," I lied. Although I had bought the house I still kept the condo so that I could spend time with Greg whenever he visited—after all he was paying the rent. Danny had never been inside the condo and Greg had never seen my house. I kept both of them separate.

Danny took me to my house and I asked him to spend the night. I really wanted to just bundle up with him in bed.

∞∞∞∞

I went to Trina's hair salon to get my hair done and was so surprised to see how quickly she had blown up like an inflated balloon. At four months pregnant, her butt was all of a sudden looking like it was trying to compete with mine and her boobs were full and rounded. Rick had wasted no time in knocking her up after they got married. In fact, she said she got pregnant on their honeymoon. When she called and told me she was pregnant, I was so shocked. I was not expecting to hear that so soon.

"What! So you weren't using any protection?" I asked.

"There's no need to. He is my husband," she said.

"That's right. I know he is tearing that ass up!" I joked.

"Bubbler, jeeze," she said as she laughed. "That's what married folks do—keep each other satisfied."

"Excuse me. I would not know," I told her.

Seeing Trina happy and glowing, made me feel really good. I knew she was going to be a good Momma and Rick was super happy to have a child especially since his children's mother in America refused to send their children to visit. She said she was scared that if she sent them to Jamaica, Rick might not send them back. He called them all the time, but based on how he spoke about them, you could tell that was not enough. He wanted to see them.

I rubbed her bulging belly, "I know you are going to be a cute ass just like your momma. And a good girl too–not like your God momma here!"

"What am I going to do with you, Bubbler?" Trina said laughing.

That was all Trina did when she was around me–laughed. But she was like my sister and I loved her to death. She wanted to know what Danny and I were doing and I told her I was not ready to settle down. She did not know that I was still seeing Greg or that I still occupied the condo. She thought that once I moved into the house and Danny started sleeping over, that I would have cut Greg off. Danny and Rick got along fine and it was always fun when we went out together.

"So when are you going to be ready, Bubbler? Don't you think you have had enough fun to last you a lifetime? He is a good guy and he really cares for you. Please don't break his heart," she begged me.

"Danny is alright man. Everything is cool with us," I told her.

"You need to stop playing. You know he loves you," she said.

"I love Danny too, but I am just not ready yet to settle down and have someone in my bed all the time. Plus Danny has plans and I don't want to distract him from what he is trying to accomplish," I told her.

"Marriage will not stop his plans and he is always in your bed," she reminded me. "So that is not an excuse," she continued.

As usual, Trina hooked my hair up. I went home, showered and put on my sexy black dress. I slipped a pair of five-inch red pumps on my feet and grabbed up my red clutch purse and sat on the verandah waiting for Danny to pick me up. It was my birthday and he was taking me out to dinner. He pulled up in a black Mercedes Benz; handed me the keys and said, "Happy birthday, babe." I almost fainted.

"Is this a joke? Did you really buy me a car–a Benz?" I asked.

"Yes, you deserve to have a Benz," he said as he held onto my ass and stared into my eyes.

It was not one of the new models, but I did not care. I had come to realize that Danny did not like to draw too much attention so although he had the money, he would not have bought me one of the latest models anyway. He always wanted to make sure that if any questions were raised, he could justify them. Just the thought of him buying me a car–a Benz at that–made me want to undress him right there on my verandah. I had dreamed of owning one of those cars for such a long time that I couldn't believe that Danny made my dream become a reality. It took everything I had in me to leave that house without pulling that man's clothes off.

Danny took me to a really nice restaurant overlooking the sea and made me feel so special. We had a full course meal as we sipped on red wine and stared into each other's eyes. After dinner, we strolled along the beach bare-footed, hand-in-hand, guided only by the light coming from the moon. Every now and again, Danny would stop, pull me close to him and plant a kiss on my lips, cheeks or forehead. There was no denying the emotions between us. As I wrapped my legs around him that night, listened to his heart beating and watched him sleeping peacefully in my arms, I knew that what I had with Danny was more than fun.

CHAPTER
ELEVEN

Momma called hysterical one night. At first I could not understand what she was saying because of the wailing and hollering on the other end of the line. The lines were also breaking up, but after several attempts I finally heard her say, "Lord Jesus, Mercedes, Andre, crashed and almost died."

"What!" I said.

"Crashed where?" I asked.

She told me that he was on his way home after visiting his parents in the country when a tractor trailer ran him off the road. His car tumbled down a cliff and landed in a ditch and they had to cut open the car in order to get him out. He suffered broken bones all over his body–his ribs, hands, feet– pretty much every bone was broken. I started wailing myself.

My stepfather, Andre, and I had become very close over the last several years. When Momma got pregnant, I was vexed with Andre and most times Momma acted like I did not exist. I walked around the house huffing and puffing and he could not say anything to me. Andre pretty much stayed out of my way for fear his presence would create problems between me and Momma. I knew he must have been relieved the day I packed and said I was leaving. Momma got fired up and tried to talk me out of it, but Andre told her that I was old enough to make my own decisions so she should leave me alone.

I also started showing Andre more respect and he slowly evolved into the stepdaddy role and I embraced the father figure I had missing all my life. It did not make sense for me to hold on to anything that happened in the past. Momma was happy with him and he was a good father to my sister, Simone. I would not spoil that no matter what I thought or felt. Andre also seemed to like Danny a lot so whenever we went to Kingston and had some free time we went to see them.

I told Momma that I would see if Danny would be available to take me to the hospital the next day to visit Andre. Although he was in a cast and was in the Intensive Care Unit (ICU) on a life-saving machine, and might not be aware that I was there, I still wanted to see him. Danny had planned on going to St. Elizabeth to check on his weed farm the next day, but postponed it so that he could take me to visit Andre.

When we walked through the glass doors into the ICU area at the hospital and saw Andre wrapped up in that cast and hooked up to all kind of machines, I broke down. It did not matter that Momma had told me he was in a full body cast, I was not prepared for what I saw. I cried for him, but I cried more for Momma and Simone. Andre had stepped into my mother's life and totally turned it around. She now had a business that was making money, drove a nice car, owned a beautiful house and had Simone in private school. I knew Momma was tough and that no matter what she would get through it, but women like Momma sometimes needed someone to guide them. Without Andre I didn't know what her life was going to be like.

Danny pulled me into his arms and tried to console me. The doctors said that Andre's condition was very critical, but if he could get past the next few days then all the swelling should go down and he would stand a better chance of surviving. I was not a praying person, but I still remember the days I went with my grandmother to her revival church. That night I decided that I was going to find some way to get God to listen to me. I went down on my knees and prayed for Andre's recovery and healing. When I was through, I felt so much better I slept like a baby that night.

After a few weeks in the ICU, Andre was transferred to the regular ward. His condition was no longer considered to be critical; however, the doctors were concerned about the injury that he sustained to his spinal cord. They said it was too early to tell how it was going to affect him. Only time would tell.

∞∞∞∞

As fate would have it, as Andre's condition improved another calamity hit my family. My aunt woke up one morning and found my grandmother on the floor in the bathroom. They rushed her to the hospital and were told she suffered a stroke. My grandmother was diagnosed with high blood pressure, but sometimes she refused to take her doctor-prescribed medicine. She was always trying all kinds of herbs and home remedies instead.

When I heard the chilling scream over the phone that day, I thought my mother was calling me to tell me some bad news about Andre's condition. There were no words to describe the agony I heard in my mother's voice. She and my grandmother had a very close relationship. In fact, to my grandmother, my mother was never wrong. Her sisters said that Grandma favored my mother because she looked just like her daddy. They claimed that Grandma loved my grandfather so much that she acted like he was the only man she had ever been with. All of Grandma's five children had different fathers.

Danny was in St. Elizabeth attending to business so I could not get hold of him and Rick was busy at work. I needed to see my grandmother immediately, but did not want to drive all the way to Kingston by myself. I was still not used to driving on the rugged, winding roads trailing through the mountains from Montego Bay to Kingston. Trina offered to accompany me.

"Are you sure you can take that long ride?" I asked her. She was nearing her seven months of pregnancy and was getting huge.

"Girl, please. You're acting like I am sick or something," was her smart reply.

By the time we got to the hospital everyone was already there; I was the last one to arrive. My family gathered around my grandmother as she laid on the hospital bed in a coma.

"Grandma, I am here," I said with tears streaming down my face.

"Please don't die Grandma, please don't," I cried.

Less than an hour after I got there, she took her last

breath. They all said she was waiting on me to go. I fell flat on the floor and bawled. One of my older boy cousins had to literally lift me up and remove me from that hospital room. We lingered outside the hospital for a while and I eventually gained enough composure to drive. Four of my cousins packed in the Benz with Trina and me while my mother's sisters rode in her car to my grandmother's house.

As I slowly drove down my old street, everyone opened up their mouths as the car passed by them. One dude even stepped out into the street just so that I had to stop.

"Oh is Bubbler, respect my girl," he said as he stepped on to the sidewalk.

"Rass! Is Bubbler that?" I heard one dude asking.

I pulled up right behind my mother's car in front of my grandmother's house and the wailing and bawling began all over again as everyone learned that Grandma had passed. The neighbors came outside and in no time the street was packed with people. Although they were saying how sorry they were to hear about my grandmother, it was obvious that the car was getting more attention. If I had driven home under different circumstances, I would probably have been excited, but at that moment I just did not care about a damn car.

I walked with Trina to her house and on the way we passed her old boyfriend, Chris, leaning against his car parked up alongside the road. He was talking with a group of boys.

"Bubbler, we should have driven," she whispered to me as we got closer to them.

"Let me find out that crotch still jumping for him," I joked.

She playfully shoved me and laughed. One of the dudes said, "Hey Bubbler is that your ride you just rolled past in?"

"Yeah," I answered as if it was nothing special.

He pulled his goatee with his hand and said to Chris, "You should see the big Benz she pushing."

"Girl, you rolling in dough," another dude said.

Chris did not say anything, he just stared at us. I twitched my ass just like I used to when I was younger and would pass the boys sitting on the side of the road.

"You need some serious help," Trina said to me.

∞∞∞∞

Grandma's funeral was heartbreaking. My mother and her sisters cried nonstop. In fact, their eyes looked like they had not had any rest from crying over the past two weeks. They were swollen with huge black rings around them. Although her baby daddies did not help her much, Grandma worked very hard to keep her children clothed, fed and with a roof over their heads. Sometimes she did not have much but she always said, "If it was only a loaf of bread I had we all ate it and went to bed."

Life was challenging living in the ghetto especially if one didn't have a trade, some education or a business to bring in some money. Women like Grandma moved from one relationship to another hoping to find a man to take care of them. All they ended up with was a load of children and no father to help. They were good women, but with no help they resorted to all kind of tricks and trades to survive.

After Grandma had her kids and she realized that she had to take care of them by herself, she started working as a domestic helper washing and cleaning for people who could afford to pay her. When that was not bringing in enough money, she started buying things from the wholesales in downtown Kingston in bulk and selling them retail in the market on the weekends. Grandma was never home, always trying to hustle to bring in food, but all it did was gave my mother and her sisters unsupervised time to roam the street and get into trouble. None of them graduated from high school; thus, they followed the same difficult path of not being able to effectively provide for their families.

Two of my aunts still lived in Grandma's house and there were always a host of babies coming and going. Being around everyone since my grandmother died, brought back the memories and made me feel happy about the day I packed my bag and left Kingston. I would probably still be living in that rundown nasty ass neighborhood with no hope for a better life.

∞∞∞∞

Danny never left my side the entire time we were at the funeral. I was so happy for his support and the love and attention he gave me during such a difficult time. Having him by my side meant so much to me. I was dressed in a low-cut, long black dress that showed up all my curves. It had a long slit down the left leg that parted when I walked. Although I was looking sexy, I was too sad to feel good about how I looked. However, I knew Danny was uneasy about all the attention I was getting and held tightly onto me.

After the funeral ceremony at the church, I traded my five-inch pumps for a pair of sandals. Trina and Rick came too and I could see the stares from Chris every time she passed by him. He and his Indian girlfriend had broken up and he was just moving from one neighborhood chick to the other. Because his parents had some money, he was able to float it around. Chris had graduated from high school and although he had the opportunity to go to college he did not want to and neither did he want to work. If he was not helping out in his parent's meat mart, he was hanging out on the street corner with the boys.

My grandmother used to say that Chris was "a worthless Chinese boy. All that money his parents have and he doesn't want to do anything with his life. He is just sitting around waiting until they die to inherit everything." One of his sisters was a doctor and the other went to university, married a lawyer and had two children. Her husband had his own practice so she did not work, but volunteered with a youth program.

At the graveside, my mother and her sisters pretty much lost it. When the casket was hoisted into the grave, they fell on the ground bawling and had to be lifted up and held by those around them. I held Simone tightly in my arms. Several times Danny stretched out his hands to take her, but I would not let her go. Momma was in no condition or frame of mind to attend to her and so she clung to me.

We went back to my grandmother's house after the funeral and it became apparent to me that my mother and Simone needed me. Andre was moved from the hospital into a rehabilitation home and I knew Simone missed having him at home with her. I told Danny that I was going to stay with Momma for a few days until she calmed down. He agreed and assured me that he would take care of things at the club. By the look in his eyes, I knew he badly wanted to take me back to Montego Bay with him, but I could not go. I walked

Danny to the car and every time we said goodbye, I held on to him.

"It's going to be alright, Mercedes. It's going to be alright. Just take care of your mother and sister. I am a big boy," he said. I looked into his eyes and I could see all the love he had for me shining through. I held him tight and gave him a final kiss.

"Take your time and drive. And call me when you reach," I told him.

"I will babe. You take care and I love you."

∞∞∞

The stress of Andre's accident and Grandma's death tumbled down on Momma like a big rock and knocked her to the floor. I thought she was going to die when she lay on the floor unable to breathe. I called Momma's neighbor for help and we quickly rushed her to the hospital. She had a nervous breakdown or panic attack—one or the other was what the doctor said. While there, Momma was given sedatives to stabilize her then she was admitted for overnight observation.

The neighbor took me back home and as much as I wanted to cry, I could not let Simone see me break down like that. I had to be tough, for her, I told myself. I bundled up with her in bed that night and prayed that my mother quickly recover and I also prayed that Andre would hurry up and get better. He was doing much better since they moved him to the rehabilitation center and the doctors said that his spinal cord damage did not seem permanent so he might be able to walk again. I was so happy that I had stayed with Momma.

I spent the week with her and went back to Montego

Bay with Danny when he came to Kingston to do his drop that Friday. I told Momma to call me if she needed anything or if she needed me to come by. She was feeling much better and I wanted so much to bundle up with my man. The week away from him felt like a whole damn year. We barely made it out of the car and through the door when Danny pulled up at my house before we were standing butt naked in the living room. He had missed me too and he was all over my body as if it was the first time he was exploring it.

CHAPTER
TWELVE

I didn't know whether I should be happy or not about what Greg told me. Two damn years–really now! I thought to myself. Not being able to see him for two years. How was I going to manage? He said he would still send me money to pay the rent for the condo where he thought I was still living, but he couldn't promise me that he would be able to visit Jamaica for the next two years. Greg got a contract to work in some country called Dubai. Hell, I didn't even know where that was since I never heard of it before. But he sounded really excited when he called to tell me. He said he had been trying to go there for a long time and thought he would never get the chance. Well, the way I looked at it, he had to do what he had to do and I continued to do what I had to do.

I turned in my lease to the condo and called my cousin in Kingston and told him that I needed him to arrange for a truck to pick up some furniture to take to my grandmother's house. I was going to give him the bedroom set and the living and dining room sets needed to go to my aunt. The raggedy-ass furniture that they had there were so dirty and smelly. The kids messed them up with all kinds of filthy things—stale food and juice, gum, piss—and on top of that they were so broken down and ancient looking.

When my cousin came with a couple of his friends to move the furniture and saw the building he asked, "Wait Bubbler, is this how you're really living my girl?" I pretended like it was not a big deal and shook my shoulder.

We went inside the building and took the elevator to my floor and when I opened up the front door to my unit, his friends opened their mouths wide. I thought I even saw saliva dripping from their lips. "My girl, you're really sending these down the lane? You know they don't know how to take care of anything in that house?" my cousin said.

"I know, but I want Aunty to have them," I told him.

"You know we can get a lot of money for these?"

"Don't even think about it. Make sure you take everything to her, and just to let you know I already told her what I am sending. She will kill your ass if you don't take them to her."

He pulled on his goatee as if he was thinking about what I was saying. Aunty did not play around with her children and although he was a grown man, she would put him in his place if he strayed out of line.

My cousin turned to his friends and said, "Come on let's take these to the truck."

∞∞∞∞

After my cousin and his friends left with the furniture and I vacuumed the carpet, I turned the key in the door for the last time. A feeling of sadness instantly came over me. I passed by Trina's house on the way back to my house and stopped to see her. I just needed her company.

"What's wrong with you? Why do you look like such a rag doll today?" she asked.

I couldn't lie to Trina so I told her everything. At first she was shocked, then pissed that I hid that from her, that I was carrying on with Danny and was still wrapped up with Greg.

"You don't understand Trina, you just don't. I love him, I really do."

My heart ached so bad, I started to cry like a giddy-headed school girl. Trina had never seen me cry over any man before and she was a bit surprised. She did not say anything; she just let me get it all out. When I was through with all my bawling, snot coming from my nose and all, she looked at me and said, "You must really love this man. I've never ever seen anyone break you down like this. No, not Miss High and Mighty Bubbler." As funny as she sounded, I just could not laugh.

∞∞∞∞

I felt like giving up the condo meant giving up on Greg. The day before, I had gone there to clean up and remove the clothing and shoes that I still had there. I threw some clothes Greg left in the closet in the dumpster at the back of the building. As I laid across the bed for the last time and reminisced on all the pleasurable moments that I spent there with Greg, I could not help the tears that slowly gathered in my eyes. I wiped them away with a towel that belonged to him. I could still smell his scent on the towel and I lapped my legs around it as if it was Greg's body. I knew deep down I had a connection with Greg that I never had with anyone else, not even Danny. While Danny was sweet and caring and was madly in love with me, my heart and soul belonged with Greg. I knew he was from a different world, one that I only heard about or saw in books and on TV, and outside of what he told me, I didn't know much about him, but my heart ached to be with him.

∞∞∞

I went to the club later that afternoon and I was in a horrible mood. Nothing seemed to go right. The bartender said we were short on Heineken Beers and the DJ said that one of the amplifiers wasn't working so he needed to get a new one for the sound system. I was okay with getting a new amplifier, but I knew damn well I had asked the bartenders to check the stock a few days before and let me know if they were running low on anything. I always like to have plenty of liquor on hand. I blasted them about it before calling the distributor. I had to put in an order right away and begged the distributor to see if he could make delivery before the day ended. At first he was trying to give me a hard time telling me that the delivery truck was already on the road and that it would not be possible.

"You know what, I will just come and pick it up myself. Have the order ready!"

"No, no, no, I will get them to bring it. Don't worry," he said.

"So why the hell are you playing with my head?" I

wanted to ask him. But he was a principled old man and I did not want to disrespect him. Plus, he would have run right back and told Danny and so I could not let my ghetto behavior come into play while I was conducting business.

After the liquor situation was sorted out and the DJ had the music thumping and ready for the night, I kicked back in the room at the back with a glass of Moscato wine. I was still moping over the situation with Greg. Danny was in St. Elizabeth, but he had called several times to check on things. He sensed that I was not in any mood for his "lovie dovie" conversations so he kept it strictly about business. Just as the wine was settling in and I was starting to feel better, Sandra called and said she was feeling sick and could not come in to dance. We only have dancers on Friday and Saturday nights now and people looked forward to the fun. I decided that I was going to have to go on that stage myself.

"Hell no Mercedes," Danny said when I told him. "You're not going on that stage ever again. I told you that the only strip dance you do now is in the bedroom—our bedroom. You are my woman now. All the men who had the pleasure of seeing you dance before—good for them. You now dance for no one else but me."

"But Danny, we don't have a dancer tonight is what I am saying."

"And we're just going to have to tell our customers that there is no dancing tonight."

"People are coming in expecting to see some dancing."

"Tell the bouncer to tell them at the door before they pay to come in. That stage is off-limits for you. Except if you and I are having a private party," he snickered over the phone.

Danny was dead serious about me going on that stage or any other stage ever again. "I don't want to see any man drooling over my woman. What you have is for my eyes only," he had told me one day.

I told him I was going to get a pole for my bedroom so that I could pole dance for him when he came over. He laughed when I told him that and he said, "Gosh girl, you don't even know what you are doing to me."

So according to Trina, I should be happy that I have someone who loves me and that I really needed to start loving him back.

"He deserves your full attention, Bubbler. Not the half-ass attention you have been giving him," she said.

CHAPTER
THIRTEEN

Hurricane Emily lashed over Jamaica with torrential rain and widespread flooding. The news channels reported that although it had weakened before passing over the island, it still did severe damage to crops and livestock. Danny and I bundled up in the house butt naked as usual with no plans to go anywhere when the telephone rang. We looked at the phone, looked at each other and made no attempt to pick it up. The person did not leave any message, and we did not bother to look on the caller ID.

I got up a couple hours later and saw my cell phone flashing; signaling a missed call. I realized that Trina had tried to call me, but when I dialed her number it went to voicemail. I called Rick's phone to see if everything was okay and I did not get an answer. I went right back in the bed to bundle up with my man.

Rick called later in the evening to tell us that Trina had given birth earlier in the day. "She had a pretty little baby girl."

"Oh Rick we have to go and see them now! I saw that you called and try to call back but got your voicemail."

"Danny! Trina had the baby. We have to go to the hospital now," I shouted. He was in the living room watching television.

"Does Trina need anything?" I asked Rick.

"No she is fine."

"Okay, Rick. We will talk later."

After I hang up the phone, Danny and I immediately got dressed and left home to visit Trina at the hospital. On the way, the roads were flooded and the sea swelled and lashed against the shoreline as if it wanted to force its way on land. It was almost impossible to see where we were going because of the heavy rain pelting down on the windscreen with the wind howling outside. We passed a few cars along the way and everyone seemed to be driving as if they were going to a funeral; no one was hurrying to get anywhere. I was anxious to see Trina and her new baby and wanted Danny to drive faster, but I knew he would not have paid me any attention so I sat quietly in my seat.

∞∞∞∞

Trina said that her baby girl came forcing out of her womb the same time the hurricane began to lash over the island bringing all the rain and wind with it. She named her Emily. Trina said all she saw was water gushing from her crotch and the next thing she knew she was pushing out a tiny body. "I swear she forced down on me just like the rain come tumbling down," she laughed.

"Oh no. Stop it," I laughed too.

Emily was so precious and tiny with a little fire about her. I just wanted to snatch her up into my arms and hold her there forever. Out of the corner of my eyes, I saw Danny watching me as I held Emily in my arms and softly touched her tiny shriveled hand.

As we curled up in bed that night, Danny kissed me softly and said, "Do you want to have babies Mercedes?"

"I don't know," I said. "Someday I might. Not right now."

"What is it you want Mercedes? Sometimes I feel like you are here with me and sometimes you are not. I know you enjoy being with me, but something is missing."

"Why would you say that, Danny? What reasons have I given you to think that way?"

"Sometimes you seem to be in deep thought like your mind is somewhere else. Is there someone else?"

"When would I have time for someone else? I am always with you, at the club or with Trina. I don't even go to see my mother anymore unless you are with me. Stop putting things that don't exist in your head. I am here with you," I said as I kissed him softly on his lips.

He looked at me, breathed deeply and said, "I have never loved anyone as much as I love you, Mercedes."

I held tightly onto Danny as tears ran out of the corner of one of my eyes. I knew he loved me and I loved him too, but my heart was still aching for someone else who I knew I would not be able to have. If I could just get over Greg and stop hoping that one day he was going to come hopping on a plane and lick me all over, I could give my heart solely to Danny. But I just did not know how to do it.

I went with Danny to St. Elizabeth to check on his parents and to see if any of his weed crops had been damaged during the hurricane. For whatever reason, I started to get nervous each time we visited the field. The closer I got to Danny, the more I dreaded for something to happen to him. From day one he always tried to convince me that there was nothing to worry about because only he and the guys who looked after the field knew about it. He said he wasn't paying them, but instead splitting the crop with them each time they had a harvest.

"They have the same interest as I have in this business," he said.

"Well, what if someone gets greedy and wants everything for himself and try to set up people to rob you," I asked him.

"I cannot worry about that Mercedes. That's the risk that goes with this business."

So I had stopped going with him.

Danny's sister, Thelma, looked me up and down when we stepped onto the verandah. We had been to his parents' house on several occasions, but she was always at work. His mother gave me a hug and as usual his father greeted me with a cheerful, "Is everything okay?"

"Yes, I am fine," I told him.

We sat down and they all started talking about the hurricane that had just passed.

"Boy let me tell you, some wind blew against the roof and the rain fell like it didn't want to stop," his father said.

"Did anything get damaged?" Danny asked.

"No just a small area of the roof was leaking. We got Tall Man to fix it this morning. The river bed flooded, but he had moved the goats to the shed over the field," his father said.

They chit-chatted for a while longer and then Danny told Thelma that I needed help in getting a copy of my birth certificate and asked if she could help me since she worked with the Registration Department.

"She can go down there and fill out the paperwork," she responded.

"Since you work there, can you help her?" he asked.

"I am not sure if I am going to have the time. I'll see," she said.

I kept quiet but it was clear that she did not like me. I planned on telling Danny that I didn't need her help. I would go to the office in Montego Bay to see what I needed to do. I had put off trying to get a copy of my birth certificate since I was 18 years old so if I had to wait a while longer it would be okay. I had told Danny to leave me at his parents when he went to the field, but with Thelma's attitude toward me I changed my mind.

"Listen Mama, I am going to make a run down the road, Mercedes is going to stay until I come back," Danny said.

"Oh, I am coming with you," I said.

"You could stay," his mother said. Thelma rolled her eyes at her mother and then turned around and gave Danny an evil look as if to say, "Bring your whore with you."

I picked up my handbag and walked off the verandah with him. He saw Thelma's look so he didn't try to stop me. When we got in the vehicle he said that I should not pay Thelma any attention. "She is just feeding into what Damion's mother is telling her," he said.

"They're friends like that?" I asked.

"Yeah, they went to high school together," he said.

I was happy she was not willing to help me with getting a

copy of my birth certificate. I wouldn't want her ass to know about my situation because she and Danny's son, Damion, mother would have had something to laugh about. I was not about to give anyone the opportunity to laugh at my expense.

∞∞∞∞

The next day, I went to the birth certificate office in Montego Bay to see if I could get help. I had gotten copies of my high school records showing my birthdate and my baptismal certificate from the church. I had also gotten a letter from a Justice of Peace certifying that he personally knew me and that I was who the records said I was. I filled out the paperwork they gave me and paid the fee. I was told that I should return to the office in two weeks for the document.

When I returned, they had no record of Ethel Long, birthed on the day that my mother said I was born at the hospital. They said I could go to the hospital and have them locate my record. I was so frustrated and didn't even know if I was really born in a hospital, I just left. As I was walking out the door a gentleman approached me and said, "You need some help my sister?" I turned, looked at him and asked what he could help me with.

"I heard you telling the lady that you are not sure when you were born or what name your mother registered you in. I can help you get a birth certificate," he said.

"I don't want anything illegal," I told him.

"No sister. Anything I get for you is legal—straight from this office. And it will be put into the records."

"Okay, how much are you charging me and how long is

it going to take? I don't have any time to waste."

Within two weeks I had two copies of a birth certificate for Mercedes Long with my birthdate and my mother's name.

"I can hook you up with a passport too," the man said when he handed me the birth certificates.

"Okay, yeah, let's do that," I told him.

I had come to realize that as long as you have money, you could pretty much get anything you wanted. "To hell with the red-tape and bureaucracy," Andre used to say when Momma's friends complained about how they were being treated by the customs officers at the Wharf when they tried to clear their goods.

Thinking of Andre made me so happy that he was getting better. Although his recovery was slow, he made a lot of progress and was eventually able to walk again. He had stitch marks all over his hands and legs and his right hip moves up and down each time he took a step. Steel plates were placed in one of his legs to hold the bone in place. The doctors said that he was fortunate to be able to walk again considering the damage to his spinal cord. Momma said that she did not care if Andre's body was looking disfigured, what was important was that he did not suffer any brain damage.

"I couldn't deal with it if he didn't know himself or even remembered me and Simone. No sah that would have been too much. Despite all the cuts and marks, I just thank God that he can walk, talk and use his brain as before," Momma said.

.

CHAPTER FOURTEEN

I took a back seat at the club and slowly sipped on a glass of White Rum and Coke. This was not my usual drink, but I needed something strong that night to help me sort out my emotions. Watching Kenya on stage dancing reminded me of how I used to have the crowd begging for more. Dressed in her five-inch heels and skimpy, two-piece red bikini that had her butt cheeks hanging out, she twirled her slick chocolate-brown body as she teased the crowd. I was having a withdrawal moment watching her. I so badly wanted to step right up on that stage, drop my clothes and reclaim my position.

Danny did not want me to dance anymore. "To hell with Danny," a voice in my head shouted.

"What was he doing anyway? He had been in St. Elizabeth the last three days claiming to be taking care of business there. Was he still sleeping with his son's, Damion, mother?" I wondered.

"Is that the reason why she acts so stupid every time she sees me

*with him—always spitting fire and trying to cause an argument with him?
No wonder his sister, Thelma, always had attitude toward me. She
would have known if her brother was still sleeping with her best friend.
To hell with all of them,"* I thought.

It had been three months since Greg left Germany for
Dubai and I had not heard from him. At the beginning of
every month, the money he was sending to pay the condo's
rent would be in the account I had set up, but no phone calls.
I could not even go home and call him if I wanted to because
I did not have a number. I signaled the bouncer to my table
and asked him for another glass of White Rum and Coke. He
looked at me surprised. They all knew I hardly drank any hard
liquor. He held back what he was about to say and went and
got me my liquor.

Feeling sorry for myself and all twisted up in my head, I
looked over at the table next to where I was sitting and saw
two dudes drinking and staring at me. I flashed them a smile
and then shifted my attention back to the stage as Kenya
continued to woo the crowd. The dudes got up; one walked
toward the bar and the other came to my table. "Hey
beautiful," he said. "Can I join you?" I jerked my shoulder to
say, "I don't care." He started talking but I had no idea what
he was saying because my mind was all wrapped up into what
the hell Danny was doing and why Greg wasn't calling. The
bouncer kept passing by the table and the dude kept talking
and I was wrapped up in my own world that I paid no
attention to any of them.

About half an hour later, the dude realized that I was not
interested in conversing with him so he got up and leave. As
soon as he left, the bouncer came over and said, "Danny said
I should take you home."

"What the hell! Does Danny think I am a child that I can't get my ass home whenever I am ready to?" I shouted at him.

Without saying another word, he just held me by my hand and gently lifted me out the seat and guided me toward the door. I didn't fuss; I didn't try to fight him; I just did what he wanted me to do. I didn't want to create a scene and I realized he didn't either. He walked toward his car and opened the door for me.

"What about my car? I am not leaving my car," I told him.

He said, "Don't worry about it. Just give me the key and I will take care of it."

He drove out the parking lot and headed in the direction of my house. We sat in silence the entire way. When the bouncer reached my house, he opened the door and once I was inside he closed the door again and left. I collapsed on the sofa in the living room and was knocked out. The next morning, the phone ringing off the hook woke me up. I got up and realized that I was still wearing the clothes I had on when I went to the club the night before. The last thing I remember was walking through my front door and lying down on the sofa.

When the phone would not stop ringing, I got up and picked it up. Trina was on the other line.

"Are you okay Bubbler? What is going on?" Trina asked.

"What are you talking about?"

"Danny has been trying to reach you all morning and you're not answering the phone. Is everything okay?"

"Why is Danny so damn concerned about me? Tell him to worry about his baby mother and leave me the hell alone."

"Huh, what did you say?"

"Don't worry about what I just said, Trina. I am fine. Everything's good. I will swing by and see you later," I said with attitude in my voice.

"Okay," Trina said and hung up the phone.

Danny must have left St. Elizabeth right about the time Trina called because less than two hours later, I heard a car pull up in the driveway and then a key into the door. I had taken a shower, got some breakfast and was lying on the sofa watching TV when he walked in. As soon as Danny stepped through the door the first thing he said was, "What is going on Mercedes?"

"What do you mean what is going on?"

"Why were you at the club drinking and entertaining that police boy?"

"Listen Danny, I am a grown ass woman who can do whatever I want just like how you are a grown ass man doing whatever you want. I am not stopping you from sleeping with your child's mother so why the hell are you worrying about who I am entertaining?"

"Oh that's it? You think I am in St. Elizabeth with Damion's mother, eh? She has her man and furthermore if she was the last woman for me to get some crotch from I would not want it. She is drama, Mercedes. Why would I want to hear all that craziness all the time? You witnessed it yourself. Why would I want that?"

"If she has a man, why is Thelma always giving me attitude?"

"Thelma has her own problems. Yes, she and Damion's mother are friends, but she has her own issues."

He walked over to where I was sitting down, pulled me

off the sofa, and our clothes fell piece-by-piece all the way to the bedroom. All thoughts of his baby mother, Thelma and even Greg went flying out my head. All I could focus on at that moment was how good it felt being in Danny's arms. I wrapped my arms around his neck as he held me close. I felt his body tighten as I dangled in the moment.

We fell back on the bed as he leaned over me and said, "I love you Mercedes. Please don't mess with my brain like that again. I couldn't focus last night. I have business to take care of and I need to keep a clear head. You have nothing to worry about because it's just me and you."

I looked into his eyes and did not utter a word.

∞∞∞

Danny told me that the police officers had been fishing around the club. They suspected that he was involved in something, but they weren't sure what so they had been trying to get information. Danny was very strict about any illegal activities on his premises. While he might smoke a joint now and again, he did not keep any large quantity of weed there, neither did he sell any weed there or allow anyone to do so. Once, he found out that a dude was selling joints outside the club and he told him straight up that he had to take his business elsewhere.

"Mercedes, I know I am being watched. But they won't hold me with anything here. You have to be careful, because they will try to get to you just to get information on me," Danny said.

"I understand," I said. "I just didn't know all of that was going on. You should have said something to me."

"Babe, I don't want you to worry. They won't hold anything on me here," he tried to reassure me.

"What about your Kingston drop offs?" I asked. "They could set up a trap when they know you are heading out."

"That's why I shift up the days each week so that they can't determine when I am heading out or not. I told the boys in Kingston that after the next few drops, they are going to have to start making their own arrangements for pick up. I am a country boy. I will run the farm, but I am not cut out to do all this ripping and running," he said.

∞∞∞∞

Danny started caressing my body and kissing my lips and two seconds later he was ready again. "Jeeze," I said. "Are you going to dun it?" He laughed as he climbed on top of me.

We spent the rest of the day chilling. In the evening, we showered and got dressed for the club. Danny pretty much had an entire closet of clothes and shoes in my house. He still had his own place, but he hardly went there as most nights he came home with me. My car was still parked at the club from the night before so we drove together. The bouncer had moved it to the back of the building and covered it with a tarpaulin. He handed me the keys as Danny and I walked in.

"Thank you. Thank you so much for last night," I said to him.

"No problem, man. I have to make sure I protect the boss' investment," he looked up at Danny and Danny just smiled and walked away. It felt good knowing that they had our backs. No telling what I would have gotten myself into if he did not care enough to let Danny know what was going on and took me home. As messed up as I was in my head that night, I would probably end up sleeping with the policeman and thinking it was Danny and Greg all in one.

CHAPTER
FIFTEEN

I had a long and restless night as I kept tossing and turning and could not fall asleep. Several times I looked over at Danny as he laid on his back snoring. I wanted to wake him up so that we could talk until I fall asleep, but I knew he was tired so I did not. He had spent the day in St. Elizabeth picking up the weed he was dropping off into Kingston the next day. He said this was his final drop off because after this the buyers would need to make arrangements to collect their loads.

"Are you going to have them picking up at the field?" I asked.

"You crazy?" he asked. "They would have to meet me somewhere. No one is allowed at that field except me and the guys."

When I finally fell asleep, I saw my grandmother in a dream warning me about going over the gully to play. She said the next time she caught me over there she was going to beat my behind so bad that I would not be able to sit down. I woke up out of my sleep expecting to see my grandmother standing in front of me with a belt, but instead I was lying on the bed with Danny next to me.

Why was I dreaming about that gully? I wondered. Was it signaling danger? What was the dream trying to tell me?

The gully was a long, concrete canal that ran through my old neighborhood in Kingston and separated our community from another where one of my aunts lived. When it rained, the water ran from the streets down into the gully that carried it away to the river. As children, my cousins and I used to cut across the canal when there was no water in it to go over to my aunt's house. The gully used to be filthy as people dumped their garbage and other waste there. We used to jump down on one side and then climb on each other's back to pull ourselves up the other side.

My grandmother used to tell us that one day someone was going to snatch us up and we would not get to come home again. She called that someone a "black heart man." She talked about the black heart man like he was so real and was just waiting to take young children away from their parents. This scared the hell out of us, so after a while my cousins and I stopped cutting across the gully and would walk the long way around to cross the bridge to go over to the other side.

∞∞∞∞

When I went back to sleep, I did not wake up until the sun was streaming through the windows. We had planned to leave before day break to get to Kingston and so when I woke Danny up he was a bit agitated.

"Damn Mercedes, sleep steal me away," he said.

"Well, you were tired. We both were tired. Can you call the guy and cancel? We could go tomorrow."

"No, I don't like to postpone on people at the last minute. That's not how I conduct business. He is expecting to see me today so we are going to go," he responded.

Danny tried to call the buyer to let him know that he was running late, and would still be coming but the buyer's phone went to voicemail. He didn't leave any message as he never did. He tried several times but still no answer. We got dressed, left home and along the way we grabbed some food. I asked Danny to take it easy. He had started driving like a bat out of hell, but I told him there was no sense in killing himself to hurry and get there. He was already late. Danny settled down and we cruised into Kingston. He usually drives his gold Lexus but for some reason that morning I went toward my black Benz as we got ready to leave. When he saw me do that, he laughed and said, "You know what, let's drive your car." So we moved the bags from his car trunk and put them into my car trunk.

About a mile away from where the restaurant we were going to, we saw police cars dashing past on the other side of the road. As we got closer, we saw more police cars parked along the roadside.

"Something's not right, Danny," I said.

"Yeah, seems like it," he said.

"Let's stop and ask someone what's going on."

We pulled up along the street about half a mile from the restaurant and asked a group of women selling on the roadside what the problem was.

"My dear, police raided the restaurant early this morning

and took the owner and his entire crew to jail. People said they found weed and guns in there."

That was all we needed to hear. Danny turned the car around and headed out of downtown Kingston. He called his other guy who he supplied in New Kingston and asked him if he needed anything. Might as well try to get rid of it since we were already in town, we thought. The guy said yes and we took the drop to New Kingston.

∞∞∞∞

I was not a superstitious person, but I believed that the dream about my grandmother was a warning for what happened that morning. The police raided the restaurant around the time we were scheduled to be there. Danny usually drove the gold Lexus and the police might have been on the lookout for one. The way they parked alongside the road made it seemed like they were waiting to pounce on someone. I believe we might have outsmarted them by driving the black Benz.

"This weed business is getting risky, Mercedes. I might need to cut out sooner than I am planning to," Danny said.

"The club is making enough money. You really don't have to do this Danny."

"Yeah I know. I think it's time to start wrapping things up. You know what Mercedes, a lot of women who I used to deal with before just want-want-want that they sounded like a damn ambulance. They would have encouraged me to continue just so that the money could keep rolling in, but you don't pressure me for anything. You're just so humble and smart. Sometimes I still can't believe I used to watch you dancing on that stage and all I wanted was just to get into your panties. But you never bat an eye my way. The person I am with now and the person I saw on that stage are two different people. I am so glad I got to know this person."

Danny leaned over and kissed me. I reached over to kiss him back, but a car honked at us and he jumped as he straightened the car wheel. We laughed as he said, "Let me focus on the road. I don't want anyone to run us over because I am going to tear your ass up in bed tonight."

I rested my head on his shoulders and rubbed his inner thigh as we continued toward home.

CHAPTER
SIXTEEN

As I pulled my Benz into the parking lot in a shopping center in Montego Bay, I felt eyes staring at me. I was so used to men checking me out that it did not faze me. I straightened my sunglasses and pulled my Louis Vuitton handbag over my shoulder as I stepped out the car in my high-heeled wedge shoes and straightened my mini skirt. My mother had gotten me the handbag on her last trip to Miami and it was the real deal, not some knock off imitation I was used to seeing girls posing with. Just looking at it, you could tell that it was expensive.

I briskly walked toward the entrance of the store when I noticed that the eyes watching me were from a woman not a man. I looked over my shoulder and was shocked to see Danny's sister, Thelma, staring back at me. At first, I wasn't sure if I should just pretend that I did not recognize her and continue on to my business, but a voice inside me told me that I now had the chance to be a bitch. I was not around her brother or parents so I could now show her who I really was.

I walked right over to her smiling and said, "How are you doing? It's good seeing you in town."

She looked at me as if she was looking at some dirty laundry and said, "I am fine, but I can't say the same about seeing you."

I cut the bullshit and got down to what I really wanted to say to her. "I know you don't care for me, but quite frankly it does not matter. I don't know anything about you, and I am God damn well sure you don't know anything about me. I am going to be around Danny for a long, long time whether you like it or not. So I would suggest you get used to it."

I was about to walk away when the bitch opened up her mouth and said, "You don't want Danny, you just want his money that's the only reason you are with him. You are a damn whore; that's what you are."

"Oh! Really now? That's what bugging you? I don't need Danny's money and if I was looking for a man just for his money, trust and believe, I can find plenty. He is going to spend his money on someone whether you like it or not so you need to get used to it. Which woman is going to give up her crotch for nothing? If that's what you are doing, you are a damn fool."

I pressed my car remote and let it beep. I straightened my handbag across my shoulder and walked away with my head in the air. "You want to be mad, be mad bitch," I laughed to myself.

When I walked out of the store with my shopping bags dangling against my legs, I stumbled into a gentleman on the way to my car. I turned around to apologize and realized that it was the policeman who had tried to sweet talk me at the club the night my head was all messed up. I mumbled, "I am sorry" and pushed past him. He did not say a word; he just stared at me. When I pressed my alarm to open up my car door, he continued to stand on the sidewalk with his hands in his pockets looking at me. I put my shopping bags in the trunk, got into the car and drove away as he continued to watch the car slowly driving away.

∞∞∞

Later that night at the club, I told Danny I ran into his sister. He said, "Yes I know. She told me. She is in town with some friends for the weekend."

"And what else did she tell you?"

"That you let her know that you can get any man you want." He looked at me with a straight face.

"I am not looking for anyone Danny I have you. But there is no reason for her to keep giving me attitude as if I am taking something away from her."

"It has always been just me and her and she is just concerned, that's all."

"Concerned about what? You are a grown ass man now. Furthermore, she is younger than you so what reason does she have to think that she can regulate your life. She needs to let you live your life the way you choose to live it."

"You're right, but she has seen women take me for a fool before and she is just trying to look out for my interest."

"Well, the way you used to sling your cock around of course women are going to want something in return."

"Mercedes, all of that is behind us now. We have each other and that's the way it is going to be. Thelma will eventually come around. Don't worry about her."

He pulled my face closer to his and said, "My fiery little woman," and kissed me on the lips.

∞∞∞∞

I later learned that the reason why Danny's baby mother was so angry with him all the time was because while he was with her he was also sleeping with another girl from their community. When his baby mother found out about them, she broke off with him. Damion was just a baby and for a long time his mother would not allow Danny to see the boy. She tried to use him as a pawn. Because she had always been Thelma's friend, she eventually loosened up with Thelma's interference.

When Danny opened the business in Montego Bay, he had the other girl living with him and was paying to send her to teacher's college. Once the girl finished teacher's college and started working, she moved out and broke off with Danny. Thelma believed that the girl only used Danny to move away from the country and to go to school.

Since then, any woman Danny took home, had a hard time with Thelma. After a while he just kept his women away from his family and I was the first one he brought home in a long while. I decided that Thelma did not need to like me, but I was not taking any crap from her. If she wanted to be disrespectful, I could be disrespectful. After all, what Danny did before I came along was the past and she damn well had no reason to look at me the way she did.

CHAPTER
SEVENTEEN

I was at home one Sunday evening kicking back with Danny and watching the World Cup matches on television when the phone call from Greg finally came. It was several months after our last conversation and I had pretty much started to wean him from my system. When the phone rung and I picked it up the voice sounded so distant and different. "Hello, hello," I kept saying but could hardly hear what he was saying. The blood vessels in my heart started to pump full-time, not skipping a beat. I walked out of the living room where Danny and I were watching the television and went on the verandah. The connection was so bad I was hearing every other word Greg was saying and nothing really made sense. Just as quickly as the call came it was disconnected.

"Is everything okay?" Danny asked when I return to the living room. He must have noticed the sad look on my face. I tried to disguise how I was feeling and cheerfully responded, "Yeah, my cousin was trying to call me but the connection was bad," I lied.

"Call your aunt and make sure that everything is okay."

"I talked with Momma this morning and if anything was wrong she would have said it. He was probably just giving me a shout out."

I lay on top of Danny as he relaxed on the sofa and he asked me, "What do you want from me Mercedes? Look at me and tell me what you really want from me." He had a serious look on his face.

"Why do you keep asking me that Danny? We have each other—you love me and I love you. What's the big deal?" I asked in a very soft tone as I stared into his big brown eyes.

"Your mother, aunts, cousins, my parents, Trina, Rick and everyone else keep asking when are we going to get married and settle down. It doesn't seem like you are interested in doing that. Every time I bring up the subject you cut me off or tell me it is not time yet. When is it going to be time?"

"Danny, you know you have too much going on right now to be thinking about marriage. When we get married, I want you home with me not running back and forth to St. Elizabeth attending to some damn weed farm. I need you here Danny; here, not running all over the place."

He was quiet for a while as if he was processing what I was saying and then said, "You are correct. I need to wrap up this weed thing. I am going to tell the guys that after we harvest the last two crops we planted, I am wrapping it up. They can continue to use the land if they like, but I am out."

"Danny, you can't do that. That land belongs to you and if you are out the land is out too. They would have to get their own land. You would not want something to happen and although you are not involved you still get caught up because it's your land."

"You know you're right. You are so damn smart. That's why I love you so much," he said as he playfully tickled my underarms as I squirmed around in the sofa and we laughed.

I held him tight as we laid there not talking or doing anything; just bundled up with each other on the sofa. Then he said, "I am going to buy you a big ass diamond ring and you are going to be mine forever." I buried my head deep into his chest as he rubbed my back.

Lying on the sofa, Danny and I were so wrapped up in our thoughts that we did not remember that we were watching the World Cup match until we heard the announcer said, "And once again Argentina is the winner."

"Damn Mercedes, I did not realize that they score," Danny said.

"It's okay, we will catch it on the rerun," I told him.

CHAPTER
EIGHTEEN

A couple of weeks after running into the police officer at the shopping center, two cars filled with police stormed the club one night just as we opened up for business. They came in with guns drawn and search warrants. When the police officer saw me he snickered and held his gun higher in the air as if he was trying to intimidate me. I wanted to tell him that I grew up in one of the worst areas of Kingston and had seen bigger guns than his, but I kept my mouth shut. Danny laughed and said, "Search my club. Go on, search all you want, I don't have anything illegal here."

And they did search. They turned over crates of liquor; opened up boxes and emptied the contents on the floor; cut open the sofa in the back office; and, even had the DJs taking off the covers of all the music boxes. They were so sure that Danny had something hidden inside the club that they would not give up. The policemen walked around the club hitting the walls to see if any were hollow and stomped on the floor to see if they could find anything out of place. They asked

Danny to open up the safe he kept in the back room, but it was empty. Frustrated, the police officer who seemed to be in charge signaled the others out the club. Danny stood aside as cool as a cucumber with his arms folded watching them as they walked out. The police officer who was at the club that night went up to Danny and told him he needed a body search. He pulled Danny's gun from his waist and asked him where he got it.

"This is a licensed revolver. I am a businessman and I am entitled to have one," Danny told him.

He handed it back to Danny and said, "We'll get you next time."

"Oh yeah, get me on what?" Danny asked.

"Don't act like you're running a clean operation here. All the Benz and Lexus you and your woman are driving. Where do you get money to buy them?"

"I work for my money. I am a business man," Danny reminded him.

All the police officers walked out of the building and stood in the parking lot for a few minutes before getting into their cars and driving away. I told Danny that I had run into the police officer at the shopping center the day I saw Thelma and that he was looking me up and down but didn't say anything.

"Yep, that's it man. They're just bad minded. They just hate to see another man prosper, but it's all good. They are never going to find anything illegal on this property or at our house. I don't operate like that because I keep my shit where it belongs," Danny said.

The raid kind of put a damper on everyone's spirit. We had to clean up and put back everything in its place. Danny threw out the cut-up sofa behind the building. "I'll just get another one," he told me. We didn't feel like doing any business, but one of the DJs started playing music and after a while everyone dismissed what had happened and threw themselves into their roles.

∞∞∞∞

After that, everywhere I went the police officer seemed to be there. He was at the grocery store, the mall where the nail salon was, the shopping center where Trina had her hairdressing shop and even at the daycare where Trina's daughter, Emily, went two days each week. I wondered if I went to church if he would have been there too. And every time he saw me, he looked me up and down as if to say, "I'll soon catch your rass out of line."

One day as I left the open-air market and was driving down the street to head home, I noticed a car following behind. Checking my speed, I slowed down and the car came up closer toward me. I was just about to turn onto my street when I realized that it was an unmarked police car. I kept going straight and then turned into the driveway of a restaurant. The car slowed down, the same police officer and his counterpart looked over at me, laughed and drove away.

I searched through my handbag and found Trevor's business card. He was one of my mother's old sugar daddies who Danny and I had run into one day while on our way to Kingston. He was now a police inspector. I dialed his number. When I got off the phone with Trevor, I called Danny. I told him that the policeman and his friend were trailing me in an unmarked police car probably trying to figure out where we live and that I had called Trevor who said he was going to get in touch with the police officer's supervisor.

"Are you okay?" Danny asked.

"Yes, I am fine. I am just tired of them harassing me."

"I am going down to that station. They need to either arrest me since they are acting like they have something on me or leave you alone."

"No Danny, Trevor said to leave it up to him."

Danny sucked his teeth and I could tell he was fuming. Trevor called back later that evening and said that he talked with the policeman's superior who said he would handle it.

"Ethel, if he should ever try to harass or intimidate you again just let me know," Trevor told me.

"I will Trevor. Thank you so much for looking out for me."

"That's fine baby girl. Just make sure you and your fiancée don't get into any chaos or give them any reason to believe you are involved in illegal activities. Everyone is entitled to drive nice cars and live in nice houses and that should not be a reason for the police to harass you. If you are in the wrong, I won't back you though," he warned.

"I understand. We won't," I reassured him.

Two days later, I was driving out of a shopping center when I saw the policeman driving in. I knew he saw me, but he held his head straight and did not bat an eye at me or my car. I kept on driving down the street, smiling to myself.

CHAPTER
NINETEEN

The general election was only a few months away and every day the news reports coming out of Kingston seemed dismal. Someone was getting murdered, robbed or abducted–women, men and children–the criminals did not care. The area of Kingston where I grew up, and where most of my family still lived, was a hot spot. The boys used to fire shots from one side of the gully to the other side without regard to who might be caught in the crossfire.

Every day I called Momma, my aunts or my cousins to get an update on the situation there. The politicians seemed to not care much about all the turmoil going on in these communities. The police and soldiers were doing the best they could, but people in these communities were tight-knit. Even when they knew who were committing criminal activities, they were either too scared to talk or were related in some way or the other with the criminals so they would not give them up to the authorities.

The elections in Jamaica frequently caused a lot of

dissention among neighbors, friends and even family members. There was a lot of tension in my old neighborhood and people living in the communities on either side of the gully were fighting against each other. One of my aunts had a small grocery shop in the front of her yard. One night as the guys in the neighborhood gathered under the streetlight in front of the shop, two guys from the adjoining community walked up on them and started firing. The guys tried to run and two of my cousins were killed. One of my cousins called me the night of the shooting to tell me what had happened.

"Bubbler, dem kill Ryan and Max," he said mournfully.

"What? Who killed Ryan and Max?"

"Di bwoy dem from across the gully."

"Say what? When did that happen? What did Ryan and Max did to them?"

"Nothing at all. They came over here and started firing shots a couple hours ago. We all ran, but Ryan and Max wasn't fast enough."

"I don't want to hear anymore. I can't take anymore," I hollered. I went into shock. Danny comforted me as I cried uncontrollably.

The killings enraged a lot of people in the community and the guys on our side decided to retaliate. They went over to the other side and shot up and burned down two houses believed to be occupied by families of the killers. The tension was so high that police and soldiers had to be called in to patrol the area at nights and frequent curfews were put in place.

My cousins were not involved in any political or illegal activities. The oldest one had graduated from high school, was working in a bank as a teller, and was saving his money to move out of the area. The other one had just started college.

The next day we drove to Kingston to check on my aunt and to see what was going on. The bridge leading from one community to the next was blocked with old drums and burned out car tires. The street was deserted as police cars patrolled the area. They stopped us and searched the car we were driving and asked us what business we had in the area. Not finding anything or any reason to deny us entry they let us go. Everyone at my grandmother's house was happy to see Danny and me, but they told us not to stay for too long.

"These guys are crazy and the ones on this side are crazier so it don't make sense for you all to get caught up in any cross fire. It's better to stay away until things cool down," they said.

"When do you think things will cool down?" Danny asked.

"About a week or two if the police and soldiers keep up the pressure. Hopefully, before the funeral. The way things look, Bubbler, since you don't live here anymore it's best to stay away."

Danny did not want to hear anymore, he was ready to bounce.

I knew too well what it was like living in the ghetto of Kingston during election time. I remembered guns firing nonstop through the night as the dogs barked continuously. Momma and I would sleep on the floor for fear that the gunshots would come pelting through our windows. I remembered two brothers who went missing and whose bodies were later found in shallow graves on the side of the gully with gunshot wounds to their heads; a pregnant woman raped and strangled–the boys who did it claimed she was an informer; men walking through the streets slinging machine guns as if they were in the military; soldiers raiding a house a couple doors from my grandmother's, hauling away every kind of gun you could imagine and arresting more than half of the boys on the street.

And, I remembered mothers crying for their innocent children who got caught in the cross fire, much like the killings of my cousins. I told my aunts and cousins if things cooled down I would be at the wake, but if not they should not expect to see me.

"No man, if these idiots want to continue we will just have to have police protection, but we have to have a wake," they all said. Danny and I hit the road back to Montego Bay.

∞∞◇∞

Two weeks later, we headed back to Kingston to attend the wake for my cousins. Danny took his licensed revolver with him and I was a bit nervous about that, but he insisted that he was not going there without his protection. I wanted to put off going and just attend the funeral the next day, but I did not want to disappoint my aunt by not showing my support. I told Danny if things got out of hand we would just leave and head to my mother's house.

Two police officers who grew up in the area and whose mothers still lived there came to the wake and parked their patrol cars at the entrance of the road. This was an indication to the guys across the other community that police were in the area. Danny and I stayed close to our vehicle just in case we needed to bounce.

The wake was more of a celebration than a sad occasion with a huge crowd gathered on the street and music thumping. When I just stood around and was not participating in the dancing, one of my cousins came up to me and said, "Wait Bubbler, you're not lively anymore. Are you really not dancing and all these nice songs playing?" he asked. I did not respond.

"Oh, the boss has you on lock down." He looked at Danny, laughed and walked away.

As usual, I saw Chris fishing around looking at Trina every chance he got. Rick stayed close to her and always had Emily in his arms. He did not let anyone hold her for too long. The wake ended without any incidence.

The funeral service was huge. It seemed as if the entire community was there. The church was too small to hold everyone and so many people gathered at the door or at the windows looking in. After a while those outside the church began to form into groups as they discussed the recent shootings and other events that had taken place within the community as a result of the election. Many people expressed how sad they were that two innocent boys, who were progressing and on their way to better, lives were cut short.

"This is a senseless killing," one woman said. "This should never have happened. These boys never troubled anyone and they never get involved in any tangling with the law."

But that was how the ghetto living was. Unfortunately, once you lived there you could find yourself in the same position as everyone else whether or not you are involved.

We went to the burial ground and afterwards headed back to Montego Bay. I was so happy for Danny's support and the love and attention he gave to me during another difficult time. Having him by my side meant so much to me.

CHAPTER
TWENTY

I didn't know if Danny had spoken to Thelma or she took the run-in we had at the shopping mall in Montego Bay to heart, but the next time I went with him to his parents' home, she was real sweet to me. She offered to get me something to drink when we got there. I politely turned down her offer. We had stopped along the way to buy food to eat and I still had some of my Cola Champagne in the bottle. She tried to pull me into the conversations, but I would not buy into her bait. At one point, I saw Danny looking at me out of the corner of his eyes and I decided that I was going to play along nicely with the "heifer." By the time we got ready to bounce, she was asking me if I wanted to go on a beach trip to Negril with her and some friends.

"That's nice of you to ask, Thelma, but I don't think I am going to have the time to do that. The weekends are very busy at the club."

"Danny could handle things," she said looking up at him.

I smiled and said, "I will let you know."

I knew damn well I was not going anywhere with Thelma and her bitch ass friends. They acted like they were so perfect and better than everyone else. I could not stand her fake-ass smile or when she walked like her feet were better than touching the ground. She projected an attitude of arrogance. Thelma had left a bad taste in my mouth and it was difficult for me to get rid of it.

It appeared as if Thelma and her friends were always somewhere for the weekend. So when we got inside the car, I asked Danny how she could manage to always be ripping and running around the place and she had children—two precious little girls eight and six years old. He said when she divorced her husband and moved back home, their mother told her that she would take care of the children for her.

"She doesn't really do anything for them. She has Mama doing everything," he said.

"Must be nice," I said.

See, that was the kind of life I didn't want. Not that I had a mother who was in a position to cater to any children I had and wipe their behinds, but I would not want to have children and then they become someone else's responsibility. I didn't care what anyone said, I was in no hurry to get married and have any children.

∞∞∞

We passed by the weed field and two of the guys were there—one was missing. I could tell that they didn't like me based on the cold stares that they had on their faces when I looked at them. When I said hi to them they answered me in their throats. The response barely left their mouths. I stayed to the side while Danny chit-chatted with them. When we got ready to leave, they said, "Alright boss. Don't worry man because everything's under control here."

"Did you tell them you're planning on wrapping up things here?" I asked Danny.

"Yeah, but they're not happy," he said. "They are saying that I am acting like a sissy and that I am having my woman running things."

"Really!" was all I could say.

"We are not going to worry about them. They have to do for them and I have to do for me. I can't spend my entire life living like this. I need more. I need a little girl who looks just like her mama–brown and beautiful," he looked over at me and smiled.

In your damn dreams. I don't want to have any little girl who looks like me because she is going to act just like I did, I thought. He had no idea the hell raiser I was growing up. No, I don't want to have someone around me reminding me of my past.

∞∞∞

I spent the Christmas holidays with Momma and I had a ball of a time. Things had calmed down in Kingston, since the election. The night before Christmas, my sister, Simone and I spent the day into the night with Momma at the Arcade. Everyone was out in full swing doing their last minute Christmas shopping. The Arcade was filled with people trying to buy their Christmas and Boxing Day outfits. A sound system nearby Momma's stall blasted reggae music. I sat on a stool and Momma came over and started dancing.

"Wait Mercedes, you don't dance anymore?" she asked me. I nodded my head, but told her I did not feel like it.

A guy selling clothes two stalls over tried to indulge me in conversation.

"Hey sexy. How the holiday treating you?"

I rolled my eyes and hissed my teeth. I was not interested in conversing with anyone. My mind was on Danny. He had not called me since I left Montego Bay the day before. He had wanted me to spend the holidays with him and his family in St. Elizabeth, but I told him I did not want to stay at his parents' house. I could not stand being under the same roof with Thelma for a couple of hours much less a couple of days. Nope, I was just not having it.

Her daughters had taken to me and had started calling me Aunty Mercedes. They won my heart over and I was spoiling them with all kinds of gifts and treats each time Danny and I visited. His parents and I were also cool, but I just could not stand Thelma's ass. Danny said that it was because we got off on the wrong footing, but that Thelma was really cool if I only gave her the chance. I was not about to give the bitch any chance to get too close to me. I like it the way it was between us—cordial.

"Are you okay Mercedes?" Momma asked when she saw me being so quiet. She had a concerned look on her face and I quickly said, "I am just a bit stiff from the drive here."

"You and Simone could go home if you like," she said.

"No, I'll just take a walk to stretch my muscles. Come on," I said to Simone.

Simone and I walked around admiring the Christmas decorations in the park and talking and laughing. We came upon a group of young boys within her age group—early teens–and one of them walked over to the side where we were and bounced into Simone. This was his way of trying to get her attention. The other boys stood to the side watching and laughing. When I realized what was up I looked at them and shouted, "Get the hell away." They ran off laughing.

Simone looked somewhat embarrassed and I hugged onto her as we continued walking.

"Do you have a boyfriend?" I asked her.

"Are you crazy? Daddy would be mad."

I said, "Oh yeah, I guess he would."

"Why do you sound like that Mercedes?" she asked me.

"Sound how?"

"A bit sarcastic. You don't like Daddy, right?"

"Why would you say that?" I asked.

"Because I see how sometimes you look at Daddy with a mean face and when he tries to say something you always cut him off. Also, you don't really talk with him unless Momma is around. You act like he doesn't exist. Daddy is always nice to you, but you always act mean."

I stopped walking and pulled her to me. "Listen, I like your daddy. But he is not my father. I never had a father around and I don't know how to act like a daughter. I am not going to joke around and be friendly with him like you do. He is your father, not mine. But don't ever think that I don't like your daddy. I just can't act like I am his daughter because I am not."

I hugged her tightly and I actually felt like crying. I fought to hold back the tears swelling up in my eyes.

"I am sorry Mercedes. I didn't look at it that way."

"It's okay chickadee, it's all okay."

Simone was growing up quickly. She was tall with long,

skinny legs as straight as an arrow and no behind. She was very smart too, and Andre did not hold back when it came to Simone. She got the best of everything.

∞∞∞∞

The entire place was so beautiful. The stores were decorated with Christmas lights and people were all dressed up in the park taking pictures. We stopped and bought sugar cane from a man on the roadside. All the roads leading to the open-air market were blocked off to allow people to roam about freely. We ran into one of our cousins who invited me to a party in our old neighborhood on Boxing Day–the day after Christmas. I told her that I did not have any plans and so I would pass through.

Simone and I walked down to the Kingston Harbor and people were sitting on the concrete ledge running alongside the sea looking at the water as it glistened in the distance. The moon casted an eerie shadow over the water and every now and again fireworks went off into the distance. We bought ice-cream from a man pushing a cart and sat down on the ledge to chill. When Simone and I finally went back to the Arcade, Momma had packed up her stall and was ready to go home.

∞∞∞∞

Danny called me bright and early on Christmas morning and I forgot that I was mad with him the day before.

"Hey beautiful," he said.

"Do you miss big daddy?" he asked.

"No, I don't," I said jokingly.

We laughed and then he told me that he left something for me in the glove compartment of my car.

"What did you leave there?" I asked.

"I am not telling you, go and you will see."

I went out to the car and opened up the glove compartment and a jewelry box was sitting inside. I opened up the box and let out a squeal. Simone and Momma rushed outside the house to see what was wrong with me. I held up a diamond necklace and dangled it in front of them as I skipped around like a kid in a candy store.

"Let me see," Simone said holding out her hands to take them.

"Are these real diamonds?" she asked.

"Of course," I proudly replied.

She placed the necklace around my neck and I felt like a queen, all I needed was a crown.

Momma and I spent the day cooking and it gave us a chance to be alone in the kitchen to talk as we cooked.

"Do you and Danny have any plans for the future?" she asked.

"Plans, what do you mean?" I asked acting stupid.

"Mercedes, you know very well what I am talking about. You have been with this man for so long don't you think it is time you all should get married and settle down."

"I am just not ready, Momma."

"When are you going to be ready? You are getting older as the days go by. Are you going to wait until he is tired of hanging around you and move on to someone else?"

"If that's what he wants to do there's nothing I can do about it. He has to do what makes him happy."

"It's not what he wants to do, it's what you are going to push him to do."

"Momma, Danny has things he is working on. When the time is right we will get married and settle down."

"Don't wait until it's too late," she said to me and turned around to stir the pot.

How could I tell my mother that I love Danny, but my brain was wrapped up with someone else? Someone who I was stupidly holding out hope that someday he would call and then he would be on the next flight to Jamaica! It had been more than a year since Greg went to Dubai and except for the one time that he tried to call and the connection was bad, I had not heard from him. I still carried him in my soul and I still believed that someday he would be back into my arms. Everyone said that Danny and I made a great couple and although I cared deeply for Danny and had great sex with him, I was still yearning for Greg.

My mother would think that I was crazy if I told her. I shook my head and laughed. She looked over at me and said, "What are you laughing about?"

"Nothing," I said.

∞∞∞∞

The Boxing Day party in my old neighborhood was the bomb. It was held two doors down from my grandmother's house so all my cousins and old friends were there. The music boxes were placed into the street and the street was closed off to traffic. I was dressed in a tight-fitted red mini skirt with an off-the-shoulder black blouse and high-heeled black pumps. I put on my diamond necklace Danny gave me for Christmas then reconsidered; put it away and instead wore my gold necklace with gold earrings and several gold bangles. I had these pieces of jewelry for a while and thought that if someone decided to rob me, I could easily part with them. It did not matter that I grew up in the area, I always had to be on the look-out that anything could happen.

It felt like old times. No one could compete with me that night as I danced up a storm. "Go Bubbler, go Bubbler," they chanted. Some of the younger girls tried to challenge me, but I made them look like they were not even trying.

"Wait, you still have the dancing in you, man?" my cousins asked.

"This is me; Bubbler for life," I said as the liquor started talking in my head. I had to put the Heineken Beer bottle down on the ground. I was always very conscious of when I thought I had enough and would not drink anymore. When I put the beer bottle on the ground, my cousin handed me another and I declined.

"Drink man and have fun," he said.

"No man, I am good."

My cousin kept pushing the beer bottle at me and I insisted that I had had enough. I was not going to put myself in the position for anyone to take advantage of me because I was too drunk to realize what was happening. Plus, I was driving back to my mother's house once the party broke up. I could not sleep in my grandmother' house. My cousins and their children kept it filthy. Even when we lived in the neighborhood, Momma's house was spotless. I was not used to living in a dirty place. The party finally broke up just before dawn and I hopped into my car and hit the road to my mother's house.

CHAPTER
TWENTY-ONE

For a long time I could not get Greg out of my mind. Every time my cell phone rang and an unavailable number came up, my heart jumped and then I would feel sad when I realized that he was not calling. Whenever I saw a tall and slender White man with green eyes on the beach in Montego Bay or anywhere else in the area, I would look intensely thinking it was Greg. They all seemed to look alike. He was still putting the rent money for the condo in the account each month but no call, letter or even a card in the mail to tell me that he was okay.

I went back to the condo to check with the people who were now renting it to see if any mail came there for me. When they told me none came, I walked around to the beach and sat down and cried my heart out. Why was he still sending me money if he didn't want to be with me? I wondered. I slowly weaned my mind away from him.

After my conversation with Momma over the Christmas holiday regarding what my plans were for Danny, I really started to give thought to our relationship. Danny invoked a feeling in me that I could not explain. Whenever he smiled at me, my heart would beat nonstop and my crotch would get wet immediately. We could have sex all day and every day and I would still want more. And when I bundled up in bed with him and listened to his heartbeat, I would feel so happy and contented. I began to think that Danny was probably the man designed for me and that I needed to stop focusing on someone who I could not have a future with. So after the Christmas holidays and I went back to Montego Bay, I decided that the future belonged to Danny and me. It did not matter if Greg came calling again, I was not dancing to the beat of his drum anymore.

I threw myself back into the routine: running the club, going to St. Elizabeth with Danny whenever he went to see his parents, and keeping him busy in bed. The final weed crops were almost ready and I was looking forward to him wrapping up the weed business. He scooped me up and took me away to Negril one weekend. One night as we laid on the beach staring up at the moon, I told him that I was ready to spend the rest of my life with him.

"I know it would seem like I am not trying to commit to you Danny, but I just wanted to make sure that I am doing the right thing. I love you so much, I just want to be with you," I told him.

He kissed my lips, pulled me up from off the sand and grabbed my hands as he started running toward the parking lot of the hotel. "Where are we going?" I asked.

Danny did not answer. He just kept running and pulling me with him. I felt like a young girl being led. He went toward his car and pulled a bag from the compartment between the two front seats. He went down on his knees as he took a small jewelry box out of the bag, opened it up and took a ring out, "Will you marry me Mercedes?" he asked.

Between the tears running from my eyes and trying to catch my breath from running, I said, "Yes, Danny I will marry you."

Just like he had promised, he bought me a big ass diamond ring. We hugged each other and cried as the salt and sand from the beach mingled with our bodies. Danny had bought my ring and held on to it hoping that someday I would decide to marry him. He wanted to make sure that when I finally agreed he had the ring so he had been carrying it around with him since he bought it.

Everyone was excited when we called and told them that we were engaged. We decided on a date that would be six months later. Trina suggested that I start the planning right away to avoid getting stressed out and running around at the last minute. I felt like my life had fallen in place with everything going so smoothly since the first day I landed in Montego Bay. I also felt like Danny and I had a relationship like no other: we were best friends, had great sex, and were very comfortable with each other. I had no idea that a couple weeks later that would all change.

∞∞∞∞

We were at the club one night, before we opened up for business, going over the bills in the room at the back when the bartender came to tell Danny that he had a visitor. He left and I continued to sort everything out and when I was through, I went outside to see what he was doing. Danny was not in the club and I went outside and saw him around the back standing alongside the wall with one foot braced against the wall as he folded his arms across his chest. Standing in front of him was a woman. I had never seen her before and when I walked up to them they seemed a bit startled.

Danny immediately apologized for leaving me alone and introduced the woman as a longtime high school friend who was in the area for the weekend. I politely said hi to her and then went back inside the club. A few hours later, while everything was under control I decided that I was heading home early because I was not feeling well. I felt like I was coming down with a cold. I went home, took some medicine and went straight to bed.

I awoke the next morning before day break, reached over to hug Danny and realized his side of the bed was empty. I called his cell phone and it went to voicemail. He had promised to move his things from his old place after we got engaged and terminate the lease, but he had not gotten around to doing so. He still slept there from time-to-time if he left the club late because it was just around the corner. Then I remembered the woman who came to see him the night before at the club and I began to get suspicious. I got dressed, grabbed up my car keys and drove to his place.

Danny's car was parked in front of the house, but everything was in darkness. I opened the door and walked right into the house. When I pushed open his bedroom door and turned on the light, I almost had a heart attack. Danny was bundled in bed with his high school friend. They both sat up and were motionless—too shocked to say anything. I ran out of the house, jumped into my car and ripped down the street as if the devil was chasing me. When I got home, I didn't know what to do. I just curled up in my bed and cried. About an hour later, Danny came to my house and wanted to talk with me. I packed up his clothes and threw the bags at him.

"Mercedes, I am sorry. I am so sorry. I messed up, yes I did, but can you just hear me out," he begged.

"Get the hell out of my house. Leave me alone and take your things with you," I cursed as I threw his shoes, clothes, and everything else that belonged to him at him.

When he insisted that he needed to talk with me, I took the gun he had given me for protection and told him if he did not leave I was going to shoot his ass. He walked out leaving all his stuff behind. I spent the next three days locked up in the house feeling depressed and refusing to talk to anyone. My mother, Trina, Rick, Danny's parents, even Thelma tried to call me and I would not answer my phone. When Trina could not get through to me she came to the house beating down the door and I still would not answer.

I felt so betrayed and heartbroken that I did not have the strength to deal with anyone. I could not go back to the club anymore to work and was worried about what I was going to do with my life. I thought about starting to take classes at the community college extension center. I had plenty of money saved up between the money I was getting from Danny, my pay from the club and what I had in the account that Greg put there each month. But could I remain in Montego Bay? I was not sure.

After the third day, I packed and headed out to Kingston. I went to my mother's house and broke down in her arms. She tried to comfort me and told me that I needed to talk with Danny. "Everyone makes mistake Mercedes.

Don't be so hard on him," she told me.

I didn't want to hear that. I thought that just when I decided that I was going to forget about Greg and settle down with Danny this was what he did to me. I had even gotten rid of my cell phone number and got a new one just in case Greg had eventually tried to reach me. I was in such a bad shape that even Andre felt sorry for me. I could tell that he was genuinely concerned the way he was making sure I was comfortable and going out of his way to get things for me.

Poor Simone. When she saw her big sister crying she was filled with worry. She reached over and hugged me and said, "Hush Mercedes, please don't cry."

I walked around the house aimlessly and hardly ate anything. This was my first real heartbreak and it hurt badly. Yes, I had cried a few times over Greg, but we never had any disagreements or a final parting. We never lived together or made any plans to be with each other for the future. We had great sex, some form of connection which I could not explain, and enjoyed each other's company but it was different with Danny. We had been living together for so long. We worked together, knew each other's family, and were planning to have a future together. I just could not believe that Danny would sleep with someone else after the way I was giving him all the sex he wanted. I really thought his time of jumping into every willing woman's crotch was over.

When I finally spoke to Trina, she was upset with me. "You said we are friends and this is the way you treat me. You are always there for me Bubbler and you just shut me out of your life. Is that what friends do?"

"Trina please, not right now," I begged.

"Yes, I am doing it right now. You can either hang up the damn phone or listen to what I am saying. That man loves you Bubbler. He is sorry. He did not have sex with that woman. She was in town and he told her she could stay at his place and he went to check on her after he left the club and ended up sleeping there. He said they are like brother and sister. Can you just please hear him out?"

"Trina, Danny can say whatever he wants to say. I know what I saw—two people in bed sleeping together. I am sorry, but we are through."

"You are not being fair Bubbler. Look how long you carry on with Greg and the one mistake Danny makes you're going to hold it over his head," Trina said.

"Please don't mention Greg. I had no commitment to Danny when I entertained Greg. It's different Trina; we are supposed to be engaged."

Trina obviously decided that she was siding with Danny and quite frankly I had heard enough of what she had to say and I told her bye. Andre told me that if I wanted to take a break and go away for a while he could help me because he had some contacts. Three weeks later, I went to the American Embassy in Kingston and was granted a ten-year visitor's Visa. I drove back to Montego Bay, went to the club to pick up some things that I had left there, told everyone goodbye and went home and packed. Danny was not at the club and it was a relief to not have to face him.

I went to Trina's house and she was still upset with me. I told her that I was leaving and she was shocked. "Bubbler you can't keep running. Are you going to run every time things get messy? Yes, there was a reason we ran from

Kingston to here because we were looking for a way out. It worked out for us, but please don't run again," she begged.

I told her I had already made up my mind. I had a plane ticket to New York leaving the next day.

"How long are you planning on staying?" she asked.

"I don't know; probably a month or two. I might even stay whatever time they allow me to be there," I said.

"Two months Bubbler. What are you going to do in New York for two months?"

"I will figure it out once I get there. I am leaving the key for the house with you and once I decide what I am doing I will let you know."

"I am going to miss you," she said.

Trina hugged me and started to cry. Seeing her mother crying, Emily started crying too. I picked her up and held her tight in my arms. All three of us hugged and cried. I drove out of Montego Bay with no idea of when I would return.

CHAPTER
TWENTY-TWO

When the plane touched down at John F. Kennedy Airport in New York, I actually felt scared. *What the heck was I going to do in such a big city?* I wondered. Should I have talked to Danny and listened to what he had to say instead of running? I continued to envision Danny and that woman in his bed as the anger rose inside of me. I dragged my suitcase behind me as I walked toward a woman waving like crazy in the air. My cousin, Sophia, came to pick me up and we drove out of the airport in her beat-up Honda Accord. She hit the expressway heading toward the Bronx. She began to ask how everyone was doing and if I had been to Kingston to see her mother lately.

Sophia left Jamaica just after graduating from high school, around the same time I left Kingston for Montego Bay. Her father was living in New York with his new family and decided to send for her. While we were growing up, Sophia and I were very close. She was the eldest of four children for her mother and most times had to stay home and babysit while her mother hustled in the market in Kingston. My other cousins and I used to cross a canal that separated our community from theirs to go to their house to play with them since they were not allowed to leave home. Sophia visited Jamaica a few times since migrating, but I was always busy and never got a chance to see her.

She pulled up in front of a two-story brownstone building in the Bronx and signaled me to follow her. We went through a side gate and entered the house through a back door with long steps leading down to the basement. It was my first time seeing a basement and it looked like a crummy hole with two tiny windows barely above the ground with partitions sectioning off what appeared to be a small bedroom, bathroom and living space.

Sophia must have seen the surprised look on my face as she said, "Rent is very expensive in New York. I am so fortunate to be able to afford this place. My landlady is cool and no one bothers me here so I am very comfortable. This is just for now until I finish college."

"I understand," I said.

It actually didn't matter to me. Once my initial shock wore off, I was too tired and depressed to even worry about how Sophia was living. I was only visiting for a while and would just make myself comfortable. I was grateful that she told me to come when Momma reached out to her. Momma said that the day Sophia's stepmother and her father picked her up at the airport, her stepmother told her she needed to find a job as soon as possible and get her own place. Within two weeks, she was babysitting for a woman in their building and then she did the certified nursing assistant course, got a job in a nursing home and moved out. She was now in the nursing program at Bronx Community College.

The next day Sophia drove me around the city. I was so fascinated with New York: the bridges, the dirty looking high-rise buildings that seemed to go all the way up in the sky, and the hustle and bustle of people everywhere we went. I kept staring and staring. I could not seem to get enough. We went shopping on Fordham Road, a busy shopping area in South Bronx that covered several miles of different stores. It seemed as if everything you wanted, you could find on Fordham Road—from electronics, to housewares, to clothes, to jewelry—you name it you could find it. There were brand-name department stores, no-name discount stores and peddlers selling their wares on the roadside. I bought some cheap new outfits and shoes. I didn't want to spend too much money as I needed to hold on to what I brought with me since I had no intention of freeloading off Sophia while I was visiting.

When we went back to Sophia's place she asked me if I wanted to work while I was in New York. "What kind of work can I do?" I asked her.

"I have a friend who can help you get either a babysitting or companionship work with an elderly person."

The next week I had the opportunity to take care of two children, ages two and four. They were so spoiled and did not listen to anything that I said to them, especially the four-year-old. They cried for everything and the younger one got upset and threw food all over the place. I was not used to kids behaving like this and to make matters worse, I could not scold them in any way. I told Sophia that it was too much for me and that I was not going back the next day.

I then tried to take care of an old lady. She was the

sweetest thing and talked my head off about her younger days with her husband who had died some years earlier. The way she smiled every time she talked about him, I knew he was tearing her ass up in bed. It seemed like she was a bad bitch too. I had a wonderful time talking and laughing with her, but right after I gave her lunch she said, "Oops, I think I just used the bathroom on myself."

I wanted to say, "Bitch, why didn't you tell me you wanted to use the bathroom?" It took every nerve in my body to clean up that old lady's poop.

I decided that I was not cut out for these types of jobs and that I would need to find a strip club. It was not difficult to find one and a week later I got a gig dancing in one. Sophia did not like the idea, but I told her that was all I knew and that it was just a job. It was not so much about the money, I just needed to be able to keep myself busy so that I did not sit around and yearn for Danny and what we had together. Before I could tell Momma that I got a gig, Sophia did. Momma was concerned and said that she thought I was just leaving for a while to clear my mind. She made it seem like I was not planning on returning. She said that Danny had called her and said he heard that I had left for New York.

"Mercedes, that man really loves you. Are you sure you are not making a mistake taking off like you did? I am sure you two can work things out."

"Momma, I do love Danny, but I need to figure myself out. I need time."

She suggested that I take the time I needed, but that I should call Danny and talk with him. I was not in the frame of mind to but just to shut her up I said I would. I got the same lecture when I called Trina. "Danny has been asking about you. You need to think carefully about what you are doing. You might never find another man like him."

Sophia was enjoying having my company and every night she talked me to death. She told me that she had a friend at work who I might like and that she could set me up on a date with him. After bugging me for a while, I decided that I would go out with him. When he came to pick me up, the cheap cologne he was wearing filled the air in the old Volvo car he was driving. I began to sneeze and he asked me, "Are you getting sick or something?"

"No, I am not. It just my allergies," I told him.

"Oh, because I cannot afford to get sick," he said.

I should have told him yes so that he would have brought me back to Sophia's place but it was too late. If I tried to change my tune, he would have known that I was lying. I cracked the car window to let in fresh air. He was a much older gentleman with a lot of grey hairs on his head. He was really sweet and said if I was thinking of staying he would help me out.

"I could help you get your papers," he told me.

"I will think about it," I said.

He took me out to an Italian restaurant to eat and I could not wait for the evening to be over. He smacked his mouth each time he chewed and when the food got stuck to his false teeth, he used his finger to shift it around before swallowing. I did not need to stay in America so badly I thought to myself. When he took me back to Sophia's house she was up waiting for me and wanted to know how the date went.

"He is much too old for me," I told her.

"That's what you worrying about—age? Girl, please. He

can help you get your papers," she told me.

"And I would have to sleep with him, right? Be his wife? I am sorry Sophia, I can't do that. Furthermore, I have not made a decision to stay here."

She seemed a bit sad when I told her this, but I was not about to get caught up with anyone who I did not want to be with.

The crowd in the strip club in New York seemed so different from what I was used to in Jamaica, probably because I was in a new environment. I stayed away from those who seemed to be on drugs or appeared to be alcoholic. In fact, once my act ended I did not hang around, I bounced.

One night, I did not feel like going back to the house early since sometimes Sophia was too much with her talking. I got myself a drink and sat at a table. A really nice looking guy standing across from me started eyeing me. He looked fine–tall and dark just like Danny. I looked over at him and flashed him a smile. When he came over to talk with me and put his arms over the chair I was sitting on, the smell coming from his armpit was so horrible. He must have not washed himself in days, and his breath reeked of tobacco and alcohol. I politely excused myself and got up and left.

∞∞∞∞

A girl I met at the club who was also working there, invited me to a "sex toy" party. I decided to go with her partly because I was curious. I had never been to one before and I was also tired of just being in the house with Sophia on Sunday evenings. She was a very nice girl from some Latin

American country and when she came to pick me up she talked my head off all the way to the party. Most of the times, I had no idea what she was saying. When she laughed, I laughed too and nodded my head and said, "Yes, yes, I hear you." I did not know if I was agreeing when I should be disagreeing, but she did not object so I continued to play along.

When we arrived at the house a few women were sitting around talking. My co-worker introduced me to everyone and the host offered me some cookies and a drink. The women were talking about all kinds of nonsense and I was bored to death because I could not follow along with their jokes and half the time I didn't know what they were talking about. Other women arrived and I was so relieved when the host got up and said, "I think everyone is here now, we can start."

She pulled a rolled away bag into the center of the room and opened it up and the women began to get excited. One after the other the host picked up the toys and demonstrated how they were used by turning on the switches and flipping them this way and that way. I had never seen so many cocks in one place. She had every color, size and shape. She even had some tiny ones for your ass! What the hell, I thought to myself. I had never heard of cock for your ass. Why would anyone want a cock up their ass when they could have it in their crotch? All this was new to me. The one that got me excited was a small pink toy to be used to massage the clit. I had to get that one, I thought to myself.

I was really getting into the freaky stuff the women were talking about. Amazingly, I could barely understand what they were saying earlier, but as soon as the discussion centered on sex, they got my full attention. Everyone at the party seemed to already have sex toys. They were discussing which gave the most pleasure and had them releasing continuously and which toy was a waste of time. I had never used a plastic cock before. But I had not gotten any action in so long, I could not wait to try for myself how they worked. I got the pink toy for the clit. That was a done deal, no second guessing.

Then I saw a big black cock that reminded me of Danny's just sitting on the floor teasing me. I was still mad as hell with Danny and didn't want to see him much less his cock. I cut my eyes at it and looked among the others. Then I saw a tan-colored one, perfectly shaped with the head bulging and soft. Yes, that's how Greg's looked. I picked it up but my eyes went right back to the black one. To hell with it, I thought and snatched up that one too. I don't want to see Danny, but I could sure do with some of his cock.

The host must have seen the excitement in my eyes as I gathered all three toys in my hand. She walked over to me with some for the butt and said, "You want to try one of these? These are great." I shook my head and said, "No I am fine with these." I didn't know whether it was just the sale she was trying to get or impress me with her butt cocks, but she continued to press me about them. I just folded my lips and looked away. What the hell didn't she get that I was not interested? That was not my style!

∞∞∞

Sophia was sitting on the floor with a plate full of curry chicken and white rice in her hand and a large jug of juice beside her when I went to her bedroom door to tell her I was back. I didn't tell her what kind of party I was going to so she was surprised that I was back so soon. She said a couple words to me and went right back to the TV and the plate of food in her hand. As usual, she was watching one of those *Lifetime Movies* that made her teary-eyed. But whenever Sophia was not working that was all she did: cook, eat and watch *Lifetime Movies*. She cooked so much food every day I swear the amount was more than enough for her entire family back home—her mother and three siblings.

When Sophia left Jamaica, she was a skinny young girl with barely any butt or titties. The night she came to pick me up at the airport, I hardly recognized the woman waving to me. Her body was twice the size I was used to and the only thing that did not change was her face. It was oval-shaped and when she smiled she had the cutest pair of dimples on both sides of her cheeks. A trip to the grocery store for Sophia was like to trip to the toy store for a kid. She bought all kind of food that sometimes I wondered if she was making up for the lack of food she had growing up. She did not wear close fitting clothes and so she looked like a frumpy woman much older than what she really was.

My first week with her, I hooked up her hair and tried to get her to buy some stylish looking clothes when she took me shopping but she would not. She actually got upset with me and I backed off. I realized that she was very comfortable with how she looked and I decided going forward I would leave her alone.

∞∞∞∞

I closed her door and changed into my night clothes and laid down on the small bed she had set up in her living area for me. I so badly wanted to try out my toys but I could not. There was no privacy and she could come out the room at any time to go to the kitchen or the bathroom. I bundled in the sheets and thoughts of Greg occupied my mind as I wandered off to sleep.

The next morning when Sophia got up to get dress for work I could not wait for her to go through the door to pull my toys out. I started with the clit massager and it made me feel like I was in heaven. Then I got my tan-colored one and it just picked right up from where the clit massager left off, releasing all the tension I had bottled up inside of me. I was so satisfied I went right back to sleep. I did not get out of the bed until late in the afternoon.

∞∞∞∞

I could not seem to stop thinking about Greg no matter how hard I tried. Everywhere I looked I saw him. Every tall, lanky, White man with green eyes in New York reminded me of Greg. I started to wonder if he had returned to Germany or was still in Dubai. I had left the check book for the bank account with Momma, but the deposits had stopped before I left Jamaica. I guess after putting money in my account for two years and not having any contact with me, he decided to stop.

Eventually my anger toward Danny subsided and I started missing him. I was horny most of the time, but was too scared to get involved with anyone. I guess I never met anyone who I really liked or made me comfortable enough to be with them, or that I was still hung up on Danny so I was not able to give anyone else my attention. Trina said that

Danny still came around, but that he looked like he was now drinking and smoking weed more frequently. Danny used to say that weed was not drugs but medicine that your body needs every now and again. For him to be smoking it all the time meant that he must not have been in the right frame of mind.

After being in New York for almost four months, I began to contemplate that it was time for me to return to Jamaica. I started missing Danny and so I badly wanted to reconcile with him. I wanted to call him but I did not know if he was even willing to talk with me at this point. I left without giving him a chance, so for a whole week all I thought about was going back and patching things up with him. Sophia was not happy when I told her I was returning home.

"You could stay here and go to school and get an education," she told me.

"I know and it sounds good Sophia, but I have unfinished business in Jamaica to take care of. I really have to go."

"Is it Danny you are running back to? He probably have a woman living with by now."

"Well, the only way I am going to find out is if I go back home," I told her.

Two days after having this conversation with Sophia, Trina called me crying.

"Bubbler, Danny crashed and is in the hospital in a coma."

"What! How did that happen?" I asked her.

"He was drinking, Bubbler. He had taken to drinking and smoking weed after you left. Rick and I went to see him and it's not looking good for him."

"Okay, I am coming home," I told her.

I packed my bags, called the airline and booked my flight back to Jamaica. When I told Sophia I was returning home, she did not have much to say to me for the reminder of time I was at her place. In fact, she acted like I was not there anymore. The day I was leaving, she told me she could not take me to the airport because she had to work and did not want to take any time off. I gave her a hug, thanked her for opening up her home to me, and took a cab to the airport.

When the flight attendant announced that we were getting ready to land, I looked out the window and Jamaica seemed even more beautiful than I had remembered. The lush green landscape was surrounded by the bluest sea that my eyes could behold. No wonder Christopher Columbus was so enthralled when he arrived on her shore that he said Jamaica was "The fairest land my eyes have ever seen."

I waited impatiently to disembark the plane. It seemed as if everyone was taking their own sweet time. When Momma and Simone came to pick me up at the airport driving my car, I hugged them and cried. I realized how terribly I had missed my mother and my little sister. And I terribly missed Danny too and needed to see him immediately. I dropped Momma and Simone off in Portmore and drove straight to the hospital in Montego Bay.

CHAPTER
TWENTY-THREE

Things did not look very well for Danny. He was in a coma on a lifesaving machine. He looked so frail and haggard I could not believe that this was the strapping man who only four months ago would lift my big ass up as he carried me to the bedroom. And when he laid on top of me his body seemed to be overpowering mine and pushing me into the mattress. I did not know if he could hear me or even sense my presence, but I begged him to forgive me for my stubbornness and my unwillingness to give him a chance. Every now and again the nurses would walk around and look at me, but for the most part they didn't pay much attention to me as I cried my heart out.

Trina and Emily were happy to see me. She was getting big and was just a beautiful little girl. I collected my house keys from Trina and headed home. She had kept the house clean, but it was just like I left it–Danny's stuff was still in the bags in my living room. He had not even bothered to go back and collect his things after I left. I buried my head into one of his shirts and smelled the cologne that still lingered with his body odor. I sat down on the sofa where we had spent countless hours making love and bawled.

That night as I laid in bed, my entire life flashed in and out of my memory as I struggled to sleep. I saw all the dudes I was messing with in my old neighborhood in Kingston; I saw my 32-year-old sugar daddy; I saw Greg and I saw Danny. I was so tormented. I realized that my past was holding me a prisoner, and that was the reason I took so long to commit to Danny and why I was not willing to hear him out and work things out with him. I cried, prayed and begged God to make Danny better and to give me a chance to make things right with him.

Bright and early the next morning, I went to the hospital to see Danny. I sat on the chair next to the bed and talked to his motionless body lying on the bed. I just kept on talking. I was so wrapped up into all that I had on my chest that I did not realize that I was not alone. Danny's sister, Thelma, had been standing behind me for a few minutes listening to my conversation. When I turned around all I saw was her stone-cold stare. I did not say anything. She walked up to the bed, checked on Danny and then said, "So you finally came."

I did not respond. It was clear that she was ready for a confrontation, but I was not in the frame of mind to go there with her. I got up and walked out of the room.

I went by the club before it opened up for business and was shocked at its condition. The place looked run down and dirty. Sandra and the other dancers had left after I did, but the DJs, the bartenders and the bouncers were still there. These guys and Danny went way back and they were so loyal to him. The bouncer who had saved me that night when I almost made a fool of myself looked at me with a screw face, sucked his teeth and walked away. He was closer to Danny and seemed to have a better relationship with Danny than all the other guys did.

Bert, one of the bartenders, was happy to see me and offered me a drink. I took a bottle of Heineken Beer and we sat down to talk. "Bubbler, the boss lost it after you left. It seemed like you shook up his nerves. What really went down with you and him because he never really talked about it?"

I told him what had happened.

"Listen man, I am not going to take up for the boss but the way him check for you, I really don't think he had sex with that woman," Bert said.

"Bert, I know what I saw, I am not stupid. Danny was in bed wrapped up with this woman and when I turned on the light they both jumped up and grabbed the sheet to cover up. If he didn't have sex with her why weren't they wearing any clothes? Which grown ass people wrap up in bed without clothes and them not having sex?"

Bert did not try to convince me anymore. All he said was, "Yeah, he made a bad move and he knew you had a key. He probably didn't think you would have gone there though. You could have given him a chance still. None of us are perfect and he is a good hombre."

Not wanting to talk about it anymore I changed the subject, "So what's going on with the club now?"

"I don't think Danny's heart was into it anymore before the accident. He was spending most of his time in St. Elizabeth so things just falling apart here."

"Did he tell you what he was doing in St. Elizabeth?"

"That's where his folks are from. But you know Danny

don't talk his business with anyone so we don't really know."

I was fishing around to get information from Bert, but it was obvious that he didn't really know anything. Danny must have not given up the weed farm like he told me he would and was spending his time there with the other guys. I didn't know how often his parents came to the hospital so I could not bank on running into them there, but I needed to talk with them about Danny's business. I could not just step right back in and take over the club and there was no telling how long it was going to be before Danny recovered enough to start running things again. I thought about visiting them, but Thelma might have thrown my ass out of her parent's house.

Andre drove Momma and Simone to Montego Bay on the weekend and they went to the hospital to visit with Danny. Momma said that she had faith that he was going to pull through. "Look at Andre! If he got better and walked out of that rehab Danny is going to get better."

I was glad that she was being optimistic. I needed that. I was also happy that they came to visit since Momma rarely visited me in Montego Bay. She said she did not like driving on the country roads so I was the one who was always ripping back and forth from Montego Bay to Kingston. Having them there with me, while I fretted over Danny's condition, was comforting.

I was shocked when Momma said to me, "Mercedes why don't you go back to school?" She had never really encouraged me to pursue education when I was younger. She had pretty much left me to do whatever I wanted to do.

"And do what?" I asked her.

"You have a good business mind. You should do business and get a degree."

"To do what? Run someone else's business?" I asked her. Momma did not respond.

"I don't need a business degree to own my own business," I told her.

I understand what Momma was trying to say to me. I had just been floating around for several years and I needed some form of direction for my future. Things had managed to work out for me, but I was getting older and needed stability. I decided that when Danny recovered, if he was still interested in being with me, I was going to sit down and really put a plan together for what we needed to do for our future.

∞∞∞∞

The bouncer who Danny was closest with had pretty much stepped in and took over running the club. I could not just sit around and watch not knowing if he was really putting away the money for Danny or what he was doing. I decided that I would drive to St. Elizabeth to have a talk with his parents. I had spent as much time at the hospital as I could all week hoping that they would come by while I was there but I never saw them.

When I pulled up in the driveway, Thelma's two girls ran out to greet me. "Aunty Mercedes, we missed you," they said.

"I missed you too," I told them as they each grabbed onto my arms.

Danny's parents also looked like they were relieved to see me too. Thelma pushed her head through the front door to look, but she never came out of the house. We sat on the verandah and I first apologized to them for running off without telling them goodbye. They said they understood.

Danny told them that we were having some problems and I had decided to take a break and went overseas. They were happy that I was back although under such terrible circumstances. I asked them if Danny had discussed any plans with them regarding his club in the event that something like this should happen and they said he had not.

"I can't just walk back in and take over. I am not Danny's wife and I think you guys need to make a decision on what needs to be done while we are waiting for Danny to recover," I told them.

His father said, "We can't run it and Thelma has her job, so the only thing we can do is to close it down if you won't do it."

"It's not that I won't do it, but I can't just walk into there and take charge. It will create problems with the guys there. I can already see that at least one of them was not too happy to see me."

His parents decided that they would have one of Danny's cousins, Charles, who they raised, return to Montego Bay with me to take charge of things and I could help him. Charles was already familiar with the guys because he would always come by the club with Danny when he came to town. Over the next week, I threw myself into helping Charles straighten things out at the club and was at the hospital everyday sitting by Danny's bedside talking with him.

Thelma took the day off from work to come to Montego Bay to see Danny and I ran into her at the hospital. She told me that she was taking her parents on Saturday to the hospital. I invited them over to the house and although it was clear that Thelma did not care much for me, she kept in check. Trina came by with Emily and she had a great time playing with Thelma's girls. For the first time since going out with Danny, I really felt like I could be a part of his family. When they got ready to leave, his parents and the girls hugged me tightly. Thelma gave me one of those preacher's hugs as she ushered everyone in the car and drove away.

∞∞∞

While at the shopping center one day, I ran into the woman who rented the condo where I was living. She instantly recognized me and remembered that I came to the condo checking to see if any mail had come there for me. She told me that not long after I came there she received a letter from overseas with my name on it. She tried to call the number I left, but it was no longer in service. She had no way of reaching me and so eventually the letter got thrown out with garbage.

"Do you remember the name of the person who sent it?" I asked her.

"Yes, I believe it was Gregory Smith," she said.

Greg finally wrote. Well at this point in my life, it was just too late. Danny needed me more than before and I was going to make sure I was there for him. I still carried Greg in my soul and every now and again I was reminded of him, but my heart belonged to Danny. I prayed every day that he would wake up and walk out of that hospital bed.

CHAPTER
TWENTY-FOUR

My little sister Simone was selected to represent her high school at the upcoming annual high school athletic meet. This was the Inter-Secondary Schools Girls Championships (better known as Champs), to be held at the national stadium in Kingston. With her long legs and graceful strides on the track field, she had dominated the 200- and 400-meter races at her school so it did not surprise us that she was selected. A couple of my cousins were very good at playing soccer, but they did not stay in high school long enough to get any recognition. We had never had anyone in the family participate on the national level in track and field so everyone was very proud of Simone.

Thelma agreed to spend the weekend in Montego Bay to attend to Danny in the hospital and Trina, Emily and I left for Kingston to attend Champs. The last few weeks, visiting Danny in the hospital and straightening things out at the club, had begun to take a toll on me. I was really happy to have the opportunity to do something fun and to hang out with my family as we supported my sister. I dropped Trina and Emily off at her mother's house where they were staying and did not hang around. I went straight to my mother's house in Portmore. I would pick them up in the morning on my way to the stadium. I was so excited for Simone that I could not wait to see her.

As soon as I pulled up to the gate, Simone rushed off the verandah where she was sitting with Momma, Andre and her friends from next door, to hug me. We hugged each other laughing. I had called Momma to let her know I was close by and she said she was waiting until I arrived to have dinner. They were on the verandah looking out for me.

"Look at you, going to Champs and all. I am so proud of you!" I told Simone.

"Can you believe that, Mercedes? I am so nervous. I don't know how I am going to run in front of so many people," she said with so much innocence in her voice.

"Don't worry about it; don't focus on the people just do your thing," I told her.

"That's what I keep telling her. She keeps talking about how nervous she is and I told her to just pretend that she is running at school in front of everyone," Momma said.

"She knows she can do it. She has the ability," Andre said with so much pride in his voice as he grinned from ear-to-ear.

"I know, she can do it. Simone just stop worrying so much. You have been training hard for this and you know you are going to do well," my mother echoed.

Simone hugged onto her daddy and for a few minutes a bit of jealousy crossed my heart. I never had a father much less anyone fussing about me like that before. I instantly became quiet. Momma must have noticed my reaction because she then said, "Do you want me to get your food for you, Mercedes? I know you said you were hungry when you called."

"Yes, thanks. I am going to use the restroom first," I told her. I walked to the bathroom and once I closed the door, I sat on the toilet with its seat cover down and allowed the sadness to pass. I love my sister and was really happy that she had a father who was proud of her and one she could depend on, but it always reminded me of the fact that I did not even know who my father was. On several occasions, I wanted to ask Momma who he was, but I did not want to hurt her feelings or to bring up old wounds. I knew Momma was a trickster and was probably not even sure herself since she was entertaining so many men at the same time. Not knowing my father left a void inside me. I splashed cold water over my face and as I looked into the mirror the face looking back at me looked exactly like Momma. No sense in worrying about a father, she was who I always had all these years, I thought to myself. I walked out of the bathroom with a smile on my face.

∞∞∞∞

Andre and Momma left very early in the morning with Simone to take her to school where everyone was gathering to get on the bus that would take them to the stadium. Momma gathered us around and said a word of prayer for her. Dressed in her athletic gears with her school colors, Simone looked like a professional runner–tall and nicely built. After they left, I got dressed and called Trina and told her I was on my way. I was not expecting to see several of my cousins waiting for me at Trina's gate telling me that they wanted to go to Champs, but did not have any money to pay to get into the stadium. I handed whatever cash I had to my older boy cousin and told him to share it amongst everyone. One of them had the audacity to be mad that I did not come to see them at my grandmother's house after dropping Trina off the evening before.

"Why are you hiding from us?" she asked, looking straight at me and turning up her nose as if she smelled something rotten.

"Who said I'm hiding from you? Why would I need to hide from you anyway?" I fired back. I folded my arms across my chest and leaned against my car.

"Well it seems like that's what you're doing," she said.

I sucked my teeth and did not answer and she continued, "When we asked you for things you don't have to give us if you don't want to. Not because we don't have it like you, you don't have to deal with us like you're better than us."

I stood waiting on Trina and still didn't say anything because it was clear she wanted to have a skirmish with me and I was too grown for that. No one was going to see me clawing and fighting with anyone in the middle of the road. Nope that was not my style anymore! She continued cursing while two of her friends standing around with her laugh as they cheered her on.

"You're not better than us. Hell no, you not better than us. Not because you have your money and driving your brand name vehicle, you can't come to our house anymore. Since you came back from New York nobody sees you around here anymore. You came yesterday and you couldn't come to see

Mama. What have we done to you?" she shouted with her hands on her hips and shaking her body like she was moving to the sound of music.

With hands on her side, one of her friends bent her head low and then straightened up as if she was doing some aerobic exercise as she laugh and said, "Whoa, someone help me please!" This was her way of boosting my cousin's ego as she cursed.

I looked her up and down. She had huge orange curlers jammed all over her head holding up the dirty looking hair weave she had on. She was wearing a murky looking, white muscle t-shirt with a picture of Bob Marley at the front. I knew the t-shirt had seen better days, but it was badly in need of some bleach and blue soap. The pair of black tights she had on with her butt cheeks printing through looked like something she had been wearing all week. The crotch must have smelled like a ram goat by now, I thought to myself. The dirty flip flops were much too small for her big ass feet as her heels hung over the back. There was no way in hell anyone was going to see me arguing with these ghetto bitches, I thought to myself.

I turned my back to them while I leaned over my car. Just then Trina came out of the yard with Emily. She looked at me and looked at my cousin and her friends trying to figure out what was going on. I opened the car door for them and we got into my Benz and I drove away leaving my cousin still cursing.

"What's gotten into her, Bubbler?" Trina asked.

"I really don't know. She's telling me that I am acting like I am better than them and that I am not coming to see them anymore."

"But she never liked your ass so why she wants to see you now?" Trina asked. I just smiled.

She continued, "The way she used to act like you don't exist when we were growing up. I don't forget the time she told that lady that she was not related to you and that you were a whore."

"I remember; straight to my face too. And when Momma told Aunty about it after I told her, she told my mother I was lying and was a troublemaker. Yep, but Aunty knew better."

Trina sucked her teeth and said, "You should ask her why she wants to see the whore. She wants someone to knock her over the head with a rock." We both laughed. Trina only had a lot of mouth but could not fight with anyone even if her life depended on it. I was the one who kept all the bitches straight when they tried to pick on her when we were younger. Family or no family, no one would try to quarrel or fight with me and I defended Trina whether she was wrong or not.

I had been so busy worrying about Danny that it did not occur to me that I had not contacted my aunt since I returned to Jamaica. Momma did not mention anything to me, but it was clear that it was something that was being discussed at my grand-mother's house. I decided that I would make sure I visit my aunt when I drop Trina off at her mother's house after the games.

∞∞∞∞

By the time we got to the stadium, there were long lines of people waiting to get in. It was my first time being there and watching all the high school children in their uniforms made me realize how much I had missed out during my time. I was not interested in participating in any sporting events and neither did I support any. I was too busy being all over the place from uptown to downtown hanging out with dudes. I spent a lot of time down by the harbor and going to the movie theatre. Trina must have sensed what I was feeling because she said, "Bubbler, how come we never went to Champs when we were in school?"

"I was just thinking the same thing. We were just having fun doing other things, I guess."

A group of girls wearing the colors of Trina's old high school passed by us laughing and joking with each other. Momma had gotten t-shirts for everyone representing the colors of Simone's school and I had brought one for Trina to wear. We met up with Momma and Andre and sat down with them. The first day of the games were the heats and Simone did very well to qualify for the semi-finals the next day.

Trina and I left the games and stopped at a restaurant in New Kingston before going home. As we sat down to eat, I noticed a woman sitting not too far from us staring straight at me. She looked familiar but I could not remember where I had seen her before. Based on the expression on her face, it appeared as if she was also having problem with remembering who I was. I looked away and started chatting with Trina as we waited on our food. A few minutes later, I saw a man walking toward us. I instantly recognized him as the 32-year-old dude I was banging when I lived in Kingston. He looked mature with grey hairs covering his head and about 50 pounds heavier. He looked straight through me as he passed and went to the table with the woman, kissed her on her cheek and sat down.

I felt relieved but at the same time a bit hurt that after the countless hours I spent lying up in motel rooms with him or the numerous times he jacked me up in his car, he did not recognize me. I guess that I must have only been just another foolish young woman allowing an older man to get his way with me. At the time, I was just looking for love in the wrong place and permitted him to have sex with me every chance he got. I realized that the woman was his baby mother who had threatened to beat my ass. She had a ring on her wedding finger and was beaming into his face. After all those years, she was still with him.

∞∞∞∞

When we got to our old neighborhood, I asked Trina to follow me to my grandmother's house to see my aunt. I knew I had to face her but did not want to get into any argument with anyone. I hoped that with Trina being there my cousin would not show her ass like she did earlier that morning. Her daddy was Trina's uncle and he always looked out for Trina and her siblings after their father died. He was a good father to my cousin and wanted her to go to college when she graduated from high school.

My cousin was pregnant right after graduation and had the baby a few months later. She continued to have children and had four and counting. She did not have a steady job and neither did her babies' daddy and both of them were living with my aunt in my grandmother's house. All my cousin wanted to do was buy the latest hair weave and brand-named clothes whenever she hustled and had some money so that she could brag on other bitches in the area. Her children's father did construction work here and there and was very good at it, but he was not interested in getting any steady work. He wanted to regulate when and where he worked.

As usual, my aunt was home with her many grandchildren as they ran around fussing and fighting with each other. Seeing her shouting at them to be quiet reminded me of my grandmother when my cousins and I were growing up. She greeted Trina with a huge grin and asked her how she was doing. Everyone in my family liked Trina and thought she was a decent girl. A lot of people in the neighborhood used to say that I was a bad influence on her. It didn't matter what anyone said, Trina and I were friends for life.

At first my aunt tried to give me the cold shoulder when I apologized for not calling or coming to see her earlier. My aunt and I had been very close and I understood how my actions, even though it was not intentional, must have hurt her.

"It's okay my dear, I know you have a busy life now," she said in a nonchalant way.

"Aunty, it's not that but I have been under a lot of stress dealing with Danny in the hospital and everything. I am sorry all of you feel that I am no longer dealing with you all. I just have so much going on." She totally disregarded what I was trying to say about Danny and continued to let me know what she was vexed about.

"You didn't even tell me you were leaving for New York, you could have told me. Your mother came here bragging that you went there to 'chill' as she put it," she said looking at me sideways and making a funny expression with her mouth. I knew my aunt was lying as my mother would never brag on her family so I did not feed into any of it. Since my mother moved away and changed her life, my aunts criticized her all the time. My mother knew but said she was not feeding into negativity anymore so it did not matter what anyone said. Momma would not fuss or argue with them.

"It's not like I was hiding anything from you, but I just left without even thinking to tell you myself. I am so sorry." I felt like a little girl once more who had done something wrong and was being reprimanded for it. Tears started gathering in my eyes.

My aunt saw my reaction and then calmly said, "It is okay my dear. I'm glad everything is alright with you."

My aunt gave me a hug just as her daughter, who was cursing me out that morning, walked into the house. She looked at us, sucked her teeth and went into one of the bedrooms and slammed the door.

"What have I done to her? Why is she behaving like this toward me?" I asked.

"Don't worry about her. Furthermore, I did not give her any message to give you so I don't know why she was cursing at you. She needs to mind her own damn business. I am so tired of having all of them here," my aunt shouted loud enough for her daughter to hear.

Then she continued, "Yes, I felt slighted when I heard you left for New York and then I heard you came back and I didn't hear anything from you. But I understand, it is life."

The air was clear and my aunt and I were okay once again. Trina and I hung around for a while longer chatting with my aunt while Emily played with the other children at the house.

My mother's family was the only family I had and so I didn't want to start any mess with them. They were not always easy to get along with and there was always some drama going on where sometimes it was best to just stay away from everyone. But my aunt had always been there for me especially during the times when my mother was running the streets with her many sugar daddies. Many times, my aunt was the one who ensured that I had dinner and took a bath and then had her older son walk me home. He would stay with me until my mother came home. Her daughter and I were never close, and it didn't matter how I tried to be nice to her, she always disliked me.

We barely made it out of the house before Trina asked me, "Is she pregnant again?" She was referring to my cousin. I laughed and said, "How the hell would I know?"

"Jeeze, when is she going to stop popping out those children? And they are just growing up with no guidance or direction. Both she and that worthless man are the same. Poor kids," she said.

"Now that you mentioned it she does look plump especially across the mid-section. Wow! Poor Aunty too," I said.

"Well it is clear Ms. Crystal is not sorry for herself because she would have put them out long ago. I bet you if they had to pay rent and buy their own food they would not be living like they are living now," Trina said.

"That's true but Grandma did the same thing for Aunty. It's just the cycle and that's the reason why they will never leave out of the ghetto or try to do better," I reminded Trina.

I took Trina and Emily to her mother's house and drove to my mother's house in Portmore.

∞∞∞∞

The next day Simone came in first and second in her races to get to the finals. Although we celebrated her winnings, we knew that the finals would be where the true test would come. Momma and Andre fussed over her making sure she was alright. He massaged her calves and had her stretching. Momma made sure she ate all her dinner and told her to go to bed early so that she get enough rest to wake early in the morning.

The stadium was jam-packed for the finals and everyone was in a jubilant mood—shouting and chanting. The sun was scorching hot with not a tinge of wind blowing. Our family and neighborhood friends took up three rows of seats on the side we were sitting. Simone was the only child from our old neighborhood competing in Champs and although it was her first time, everyone was so proud of her. My cousins and their friends, even those attending other high schools, were there to cheer for Simone. She was the favorite for the 200-meter sprint race for her age group and as expected she won with ease.

She came in second in the 400-meter race in the semi-finals and was up against some other runners who were more experienced than her. This was the race that was going to test her ability. Everyone was literally sitting on the edge of their seats as they waited for the gun to go off. Ready, set, boom … someone false started! We all craned our necks to see who it was hoping that it was not Simone. When everyone realized it was not her, we all shouted for joy. Then the race began and it seemed like she was lagging behind everyone else until they turned the corner. She pulled away from the group and launched toward the finish line with two other girls hot on her heels. Just under the 50-meter mark, both girls seemed to gather strength and pulled in front of her. Simone was third to cross the finish line. It did not matter as we all shouted for joy.

After the games, we left the stadium and went by my grandmother's house to celebrate. That was the place to be because we could put the jukeboxes on the sidewalk and play music and dance without the neighbors complaining. Momma couldn't do this at her house. I had so much fun, I forgot about Danny being in the hospital and all that I had going on in Montego Bay until Trina asked me what time we were leaving in the morning. Rick had been calling her nonstop trying to check up on her. He was always uncomfortable with her going to Kingston without him and was even more uncomfortable whenever she stayed overnight. We had been in Kingston for three days and he was really working her nerves.

"Tell Rick he doesn't have to worry, he got that crotch locked down. No one else is going to smell it, much less see or feel it," I told her.

"God, I wish he would just stop," Trina said sounding frustrated.

"What is Rick worrying about, the Chinese boy, Chris? Tell him Chris can't hold you anymore now that you have experience being with him. Do you want me to talk with him?"

She laughed and then said, "No, I will handle him when we get home tomorrow."

"Okay Mama, go on with your bad self. Just make sure you don't give that man a heart attack because I know you're going to throw that ass up on him and he is going to forget that he is mad with you."

"You are such a freaking mess. All you think about is sex."

That was so far from the truth, I had not gotten any in a long while. I was trying really hard to forget about Greg and praying and hoping every day for Danny to get well. I had no interest in getting together with anyone else.

The next morning bright and early, we hit the road back to Montego Bay.

CHAPTER
TWENTY-FIVE

As I stood in front of the man I was vowing to spend the rest of my life with for better, for worst and everything in between, my heart skipped a beat. He looked straight into my eyes and his smile warmed my heart. I could not wait for our wedding ceremony to be over with and have Danny home in my arms kissing me all over with those big juicy lips. After today, we would be together forever and nothing or no one was going to come between us. The pastor said, "I now pronounce you man and wife, you may now kiss the bride." Everyone cheered as Danny held me and kissed me like he did not want to stop. As soon as he released his hold on me, a commotion began at the back of the church.

We looked over just in time to see two men walking toward the pulpit with guns drawn. Before anyone could do anything Danny was lying on the ground bleeding from gunshot wounds to his chest. I flung myself on top of him trying to use my body to stop the bleeding. I heard voices screaming all around me with pain and anguish, but I could not see anyone. The bright and sunny day had suddenly turned pitch black. Amidst the noise and commotion someone picked me up; brought me home; removed my blood-stained wedding dress; and, gave me a bath. I was handed some pain killers which I obediently swallowed and I was put into bed. As I swayed in and out of consciousness, I prayed that this was all a dream. I would wake up from it with Danny right beside me caressing my body as he tries to get me arouse. I slowly drifted off to sleep.

∞∞∞∞

The day Danny woke up from his long rest after the car accident, I was sitting at his bedside. I had spent every waking hour of the last month while he was in a coma helping Charles to run the club and being at the hospital. When he looked over and saw me, he mumbled, "Mercedes, I knew you would come."

Once Danny was well enough to leave the hospital, I took him home and nourished him back to health. As he got stronger, we would leave home before the sun came out every morning to jog along the beach. I wanted to make sure that he was healing not only mentally but also physically. Danny was a fighter and in no time he was back to his normal self. Our relationship had strengthened so much that it was not just about sex all the time, but where we were heading in the future.

We started planning our wedding and I just wanted to settle down with him and give him the daughter he talked so much about. Every time he saw Emily, he would brighten up and you could tell that he was wishing for his own little girl with me. He spoiled her rotten with all kinds of gifts and treats.

We did not want to have a large wedding, but before we knew it the list was running over a hundred—we could not leave anyone out. Trina was my matron-of-honor and my bridesmaids were my cousin, Sophia, who I stayed with while I was in New York and Thelma, Danny's sister. The groom's men were Danny's friends. His son, Damion, and my sister, Simone were the junior bride and groom. Emily was the flower girl and one of my cousin's son was the ring bearer. I was very excited about my wedding and wanted the day to be perfect.

∞∞∞∞

During the four months that I was in New York, Danny had gotten deep into the weed business. He had aligned himself with some people he had no business getting involved with. Before I left, he had said that he was pulling out of the farming, but instead when I left he had expanded and was supplying to people he should have stayed away from. After things fell back into place for us, Danny decided that he was cutting out for good. No one was happy to hear this—his farming partners or his buyers. But he told them he had made up his mind and was ending the business and focusing on starting his family.

∞∞∞∞

I awoke the morning after my wedding unsure of my future. Danny was gone and I was now a widow. I spent only a few minutes being married to the man who I thought was going to be with me forever. I heard talking inside the house, but did not feel like getting out of bed. I pulled the covers over my head. My mother came to the door a couple of times and I heard someone asked, "Is she still sleeping?" I pulled the covers tighter.

When I finally dragged myself out of bed, Momma, Andre, Simone and Sophia were at the house with me. They seemed relieved that I finally got up and Momma instantly started hovering over me. She got me breakfast but I could not eat although my stomach was rumbling. She wanted to know if there was anything I needed her to do. I didn't even know what needed to be done or where to start.

The days immediately following Danny's death were difficult. Momma stayed with me and Andre took Simone back to Kingston so that she could attend school. Sophia returned to New York promising to return for the funeral. I dragged myself around every day going through the motions of answering questions from the police to planning Danny's funeral.

The police came to the house several times asking me all kinds of questions. They wanted me to tell them what the shooters looked like and if Danny had any enemies I was aware of. They also talked with Danny's parents and anyone who was willing to give information. The killers were not wearing masks or any disguise so everyone at the wedding saw what they looked like. After several interviews and many more hours of answering the same questions, it seemed as if they did not have any leads as to who the killers were. It also appeared that those who might know them just kept quiet.

Pictures of Danny and I were all over the news and on the front page of all the major newspapers. As a result, everywhere I went people would immediately recognize me. Some would come up to me and say how sorry they were and others just stared. The most difficult task was identifying the body at the morgue before the autopsy and making the funeral arrangements. My mother went to the morgue with me and I was so grateful to have her support. I screamed when I saw Danny's stiff body lying on the autopsy table. My mother held onto me and slowly guided me outside. I woke up most nights gasping for breath as the nightmares from the shooting tormented me.

∞∞∞∞

Danny's funeral was sad–very sad. I was hurting and grieving so much that it felt like someone had taken a knife and ripped my heart out. His parents looked like they had aged 10 years and Thelma was a total wreck. Even the dress she wore to the funeral looked like a mess. Thelma and I had finally become close during Danny's long stay in the hospital and recovery at home. She no longer saw me as a gold digger, but someone who cared deeply for her brother. He was buried in St. Elizabeth in their family's burial ground. After the funeral, I told his parents that I would sort out his affairs and make sure that I gave them their fair share. Danny did not have a will, but I was not caught up on possessions.

Sophia begged me to leave Montego Bay and return with her to New York and Momma begged me to return to Kingston.

"Mercedes, you can't stay here. Come back with me to New York," Sophia said.

"I am not leaving. I am not afraid of anyone."

"You don't know who killed Danny. You don't know what Danny was involved in that led to his death."

"You are correct. I don't know who killed Danny, but I am not leaving until I find out."

"If you don't want to go to New York, come back to Portmore with me," Momma said.

"To Portmore to do what, Momma? This is where I live. I am not leaving."

"Mercedes, why are you being so stubborn?"

"Listen, I am not leaving so just let's drop the subject."

Momma and Sophia feared that Danny's killers would come for me next. But I was hell bent on staying. I had run too many times in my life and was not about to do so again. I was not leaving Montego Bay until I got justice for Danny. He got mixed up in some dealings that he had no business getting involved with, but he was a good guy and I felt like he did not deserve to die the way he did. He was taken out on one of the happiest days of his life.

I left the burial grounds that evening vowing that I would not rest until I personally dealt with those who took Danny away from me. After all the interviews and evidence collected by the police, it appeared as if the case was just set aside like countless others. So I decided that I was taking matters into my own hands. If I had to resort to my survival skills learned from living in the inner-city ghetto of Kingston that was what I was going to do.

The next day, I went to the beauty store and bought three wigs—a black, a blond and a cinnamon brown. I bought every color tights they had in the store and I left and went shopping in the mall and got some low-cut, halter top blouses showing my belly skin. I went home and took out my hair weave, cut my hair off and colored the stubbles in a bright red color. The next day, I got dressed as I normally would, put on one of my wigs and went shopping for a beat-up Ford car. I was a woman on a mission.

∞∞∞∞

I pulled my gun from my handbag as the voice said, "Who goes there?" I tried to hide behind my Benz with the gun in my hand, thinking that an intruder was on the club premises. I was surprised to see that it was only the bouncer; the one who was very close to Danny. When he realized it was me and saw my outfit he let out a long laugh. I had not heard any of the employees laugh since Danny's funeral so I knew that I must have looked like a hot mess. I was wearing a five-inch red platform sandal, a pair of green tights, a red and green blouse showing my mid-section with a yellow purse clutched under my arms. I was getting ready to cover the Ford car with the tarpaulin and to leave in my Benz when he came through the back door of the club. I had locked the club earlier and left, but he must have returned. He had a key. I had told everyone that I was storing the car for one of my friends.

"What is going on Bubbler? Why are you dressed like this and driving that beat-up car?" the bouncer asked. I had no choice but to let him in on my secret. I needed to know who was responsible for Danny's killing. I had learned that the prostitutes on the street usually knew everything that went on. I needed to mingle with them in order to get information. I didn't know anything much about the bouncer other than the fact that he was very loyal to Danny and was probably the only person I could trust.

"I can help you. I have an idea of where to find the punks," he said.

"How come you never said anything to the police? They asked everyone if they had any information but you just kept quiet." I was so furious.

"Listen Bubbler, I have two little boys and their mama who depends on me. Danny was like a brother to me, and I told him not to get involved with those people but he did not listen. If he had just continued to stay low with his weed business everything would have been alright. I cannot put my family in jeopardy. You know how it works? If I had given the cops any information, I would have been next," the bouncer said.

"You knew about his weed business? I thought no one knew."

"I went to primary school with Danny, but my parents did not have much so I sponged off him. His daddy was making loads of money working with the bauxite factory. We went to high school together too and most times, I would have been hungry if Danny didn't share his lunch money with me. I didn't have to ask, he just split it. So when he came to Mo-Bay and decided he was opening up the club and asked me to come, I couldn't refuse. Furthermore, I had nothing going on for me in St. Elizabeth. Danny didn't hide anything from me. That was why I was so mad with you after you left, because Danny really cared for you. He knew he was wrong, but you never gave him the chance, you just ran off. He did some crazy stuff after you left, Bubbler."

I couldn't say anything. I just sat staring at him. If I had known all of this I would have let the bouncer continue to take charge while Danny was in the hospital. But I never got close to any of the dudes working at the club. Furthermore, once Danny and I became a couple they all kept their distance except for Bert, the bartender. He would talk with me every now and again. In the one month that I had Danny's cousin, Charles, helping me, he robbed the club in every way he could. First, he was giving me receipts that I damn well sure knew he did not get any liquor for and then money started going missing from the safe. After Danny was released from the hospital, I took over control again and Charles went back to St. Elizabeth driving a Toyota Camry.

∞∞∞∞

"This is what I am going to do Bubbler," I snapped back to the business at hand on hearing the bouncer's voice.

"I am going to get the exact location of each of the punks and I will pass on the information to you. Running in this getup is not going to get you anywhere. When I give you the information whatever you choose to do is on you. I love Danny, but I am not taking any role into bumping anyone off and neither will I put myself in the position for any retaliation against me and my family. I need to be here for my sons," he told me.

"I am cool with that. I will take care of them because I have nothing to lose. I just need information," I said.

"Oh, one thing I will help you to do—torch that weed field so that no one else benefits. I was thinking of doing so this weekend and wouldn't mind if you want to roll with me."

After we closed the club on Saturday night, the bouncer and I rolled out of Montego Bay in his pickup truck toward

St. Elizabeth. He said that was the best time because the guys who attended to the field did not go there on Sunday mornings.

"They were too lazy to get up after drinking and playing dominoes at the bar all night."

"Is that right?"

"Oh yes!"

We stopped at the gas station and bought several five-gallon bottles of gasoline.

When we arrived at the field, it was pitch black over the hills and even the light shining from the pickup truck was not enough so the bouncer pulled out two flash lights. We both took bottles of gasoline and walked around the first two plots and poured the gasoline along the perimeter around the roots of the plants. They looked like they were ready to be harvested. The bouncer took the remaining bottle to a plot further down and told me to get into the truck. After he poured the gasoline on that plot, he lit it and then quickly ran to the others and lit them. He backed the truck down the road and waited until smoke rose into the sky before driving away.

I wished I was able to see the expression on Danny's partners face when they realized someone had torched the weed field. Better yet, I wondered what the reaction was going to be when the buyer was told that they didn't have any weed to sell him. They thought taking out Danny was going to make the operation continue. They were dead wrong. I was selling that land to the first bidder and they would have to take their business elsewhere. We drove back to Montego Bay and I was so tired I went right into my bed without even undressing.

CHAPTER
TWENTY-SIX

The bouncer wasted no time in getting information on Danny killers' whereabouts. Two weeks after torching the weed field people began to talk. The bouncer knew exactly who the killers were and the circle of people they ran with, but did not know who was in charge or issued the orders. I told him that all I needed was access to the killers and that I would take it from there.

The first punk was a local taxi driver and it was very easy getting to him. He was in a bar he frequently visited when he was through working, drinking and running his mouth. I walked in dressed in a tight pair of jeans, high-heeled bright orange pumps and an orange shirt with its ends tied at the front and the first few buttons opened. I had on my blond wig and a pair of sunglasses. It was already dusk but the sunglasses served as a disguise and to grab their attention. It worked. As soon as I walked in the bar all the men sitting at the counter turned and looked at me. I slowly walked up making sure I went close to my target. He actually shifted his chair to make room for me. I ordered a Rum Cream and started slowly sipping on my glass. In no time my neighbor started running his mouth telling me how sexy I looked. I flirted back with him.

"You are new in town? I have never seen you around here before," he said

That was all I needed to hear. I did not want to risk anyone recognizing me since Danny's and my pictures were all over the papers after the shooting. So hearing him say that gave me the ammunition I needed. Before long, he tuned out the other guys and was totally engrossed in me. After I was done seducing him with my voice and facial expressions, he gave me his number to call him so that we could hook up. I walked out of that bar swinging my behind. Mission one accomplished. I now needed to figure out mission two–where and how I was going to bump him off.

The next day I bought a new phone and called my first punk's number. After I hung up the phone, I knew I had him jerking off. I could hear his voice cracking up and his heavy breathing over the line. I figured I would tease him some more before making my move. I wanted to make sure that when we finally hooked up all he had on his mind was having sex with me. So for the next couple of nights I called him and messed with his brain. It must have been the best phone sex he had ever had. I could actually hear the tension in his voice.

I drove my old Ford car to the strip along the beach, where I first met Greg and where Danny took me out to dinner that night when he bought me the Benz, and parked it along the roadside. I walked to the shopping center about a mile away and took a cab to downtown where I was meeting up with punk number one. This time I was wearing my black wig, a red mini skirt and tight-fitting black blouse with splashes of red and white and a pair of high-heeled black pumps. When his Toyota Corolla with dark tinted windows pulled up alongside the curb, I wasted no time in getting into the passenger's seat. Again, it was dusk but I had my sunglasses on. He asked what I had in mind and I told him that we could grab some food and relax on the beach. We sat on the sand and it was quiet and peaceful with only the occasional sound of cars whipping by. I had my gun in my purse and when the punk made his move I was ready for him.

"Take off your clothes. You look so sexy; I want to see what you have packing under those pants," I said.

He fed right into my trap and feeling so good about what he had going on, dropped his pants and his underwear in one. I rubbed up on him and started unbuttoning his shirt as he started rubbing my behind to pull my mini skirt up.

"Patience," I told him. "Let me enjoy drooling over your sexy body."

He stood there grinning from ear-to-ear. The moon was high in the sky, but we were hidden by the mangroves growing along the beach. I pulled my mini skirt up and acted like I was about to take it off when I said, "Oh, I have a condom in my purse. I come prepared because I don't ride bare back."

I reached into the car, grabbed my purse and as soon as I opened it, a bullet went straight into the punk's chest. He covered the spot with his palm and before he could do or say anything, I sent another and then another into his chest. I watched as he fell to the ground and looked up at me with his mouth wide open. I put another through his brain and said, "That's for my husband."

I put the gun back into my purse, pulled down my skirt and walked through the mangroves to my old Ford car parked along the roadside and drove away. The next day his naked body was found on the beach and word quickly spread that the punk was killed by a prostitute. Some said that he did not want to pay her and others said that she robbed him. The police rounded up several women who frequently hung out on a strip along the beach that everyone said was a hot spot for prostitution. They took them into the station for questioning, but released them when they could not get any information from any of them. With no witnesses or any clue left behind at the scene, his death became just another unsolved murder.

∞∞∞∞

The bouncer said that I should wait for things to cool down and for people to stop talking before making my move on the next punk. I had to make sure that I did a clean job and left no trace that would get back to me. The bouncer told me where the other punk frequented and I took my time studying him. He played soccer on a ball field but always seemed to have a girl around him. He also frequented a club in the area but she was also always with him. I continued watching him and patiently waited for the chance to get close. He was at the club one night and got into an argument with his girl over a man who was checking her out. He started roughing her up and she left with one of her girlfriends. I sat around and waited until he got ready to leave and then walked out behind him.

As soon as he got into his car, I opened the passenger's door and jumped in.

"What do you want?" he shouted at me.

"I need a ride," I said.

"You need a ride and you just jump into my car without asking. Who do you think you are? Get the hell out!"

I put my gun to his ears and said, "Drive before I blow out your brain here."

Shocked, he started the car and drove it out the parking lot and asked where I wanted to go.

"Just keep driving," I said.

He cleared the town and as we headed toward a thick bushy area I told him to pull off the main road onto a dirt road. The road led toward a lonely part of the beach that no one used. I ordered him to get out of the car. I needed to get information from the punk as to who hired them to kill my husband, but he was not willing to snitch.

After he got out the car, I demanded that he lay on the ground and I took a piece of rope I had in my handbag to tie his hands. He attempted to wrestle with me and I put a shot into one of his legs. He was a scrawny looking man, but I was not giving him any chances to overpower me. I had to show him that I was not playing a game—I was in control. It seemed like he did not want to tell me who killed Danny because he was scared of that person. I made him scared of me so I gun butted him. He laid on the sand bleeding from his head, but he still would not talk.

I held the gun to the punk's head and demanded that he told me who had paid them to killed Danny. The punk was much harder to deal with than the other one. He was not willing to talk even when I had his ass tied up and the gun in his mouth. I walked away trying to figure out how I could get him to open up. I just did not want to bump him off without having information on who paid for the hit on Danny's life.

"Either you tell me or I am going to take your whole damn family out, starting with your mother," I threatened.

"I will get them one-by-one just like I got you," I taunted him.

I must have really gotten to his head because I didn't have to say another word. The name came spitting out his mouth, "It is Tony who owns the plaza," he said.

I put a bullet through his head and watched him slumped over into the sand. I dragged his body to a cliff running along the sea and used the rope to tie a large rock to one end and wrap the other end around his neck. Then I rolled his body off the cliff and watched as it sank below the sea before walking away. I drove away in his car and parked it at the ball field. I made sure I left no prints or evidence inside before walking to my beat-up Ford car parked along the roadside.

As soon as I pulled away and got on the main road, the rain came tumbling down. It poured like it didn't want to stop. I smiled as I thought how perfect its timing was. All traces of blood or skid marks in the sand would be washed away by the rain. I drove home feeling accomplished and poured myself a tall glass of Vodka and bundled up on the sofa. I flipped on the TV and scrolled through the channels, but was knocked out before I had the chance to really watch anything. Two days later, the punk was reported missing and his car towed from the ball field.

∞∞∞∞

When I told the bouncer that Tony hired the hit on Danny, he was shocked. "Damn, Bubbler; Tony, really! I didn't even know Tony was dealing," he said.

"Where did he get the money to build the shopping plaza?" I asked.

"He is from money. His father is a high-profile politician and his mother's family is the Syrians who own the block factory and the trucking company in town."

"Well, the money is either drying up or not coming in as everyone thought," I said.

"He had wanted Danny to sell him his land and Danny said no. Bubbler, he killed Danny for the land, and not the weed. I was focusing on a whole different set of people who those two fools used to run with."

"I think it's the land and the weed. Tony has the money to buy any land he wants, but Danny's land is perfect where it is for growing weed. Danny must have told Tony he was cutting out and so Tony wanted to take control. He was probably pressing Danny to sell him the land."

I knew we were just guessing and trying to figure out what was the root of everything, but it made perfect sense. If Danny was supplying Tony and he was closing shop, it would have been beneficial to Tony to control the whole operation. I had a bigger problem dealing with than I originally thought. I thought I was dealing with a weed dealer who wanted to be greedy and bumped my husband off, but now I realized I was dealing with someone who had money, influence and power.

"Bubbler, just forget about him. Life goes on. I know you want to get even, but he will get his day. Please just forget about him."

I could not forget about Tony. The more I thought about everything the more I got angry. He had so much money and power, why kill another man for what he had? I kept questioning myself. That night I literally started plotting on how I was going to get to Tony. I had made up my mind that I was going to kill him. There was no way I could continue living knowing that the person responsible for my husband's death was still walking around. No, Tony had to die. That's what had to happen!

∞∞∞∞

I woke up in the middle of the night screaming and shouting. I dreamed that I was covered in blood and the more I tried to stop the blood from covering me the more it was flowing. Cold sweat washed over me and my heart was pumping when I awoke from my sleep and sat up in the bed. I could not sleep at nights. I was tormented. I was constantly dreaming about Danny's death and I could not seem to get it out of my mind.

When I told Trina about the dreams with Danny, she said that I probably needed to get rid of the club and try to start a new life. The club, she said was always going to be a link to Danny and if I continue to hold on to it, I would never be able to let him go. I was planning on getting rid of the club. In fact, I was planning on leaving Montego Bay for good, but I just could not–not yet anyway. I had so much anger in me that I just wanted to see Tony dead.

I drove to St. Elizabeth one Sunday to visit Danny's grave and as I lay on the cold concrete and poured out my heart to him, a butterfly flew from out the bushes and lay right on my chest. I watched the butterfly as it laid there for a few seconds before flying away. An unexplainable calm came over me. I left the graveside and went by Danny parent's house. They were happy to see me and it seemed like they were trying to pull themselves together. Thelma too seemed much better than the last time I saw her at the funeral. She gave me a hug and asked how I was holding up.

"It's hard, but I am hanging in there," I told them.

Danny's father said, "Mercedes, I know you love my son. Take your time and grieve but remember you have a lot of years left. This is not the end of your life."

I knew he meant well, but I thought it was too early for him to be telling me that. Furthermore, I didn't expect to hear that from any of Danny's family. It made me feel like they wanted me to just quickly move on and forget about what I had with their son. I did not respond, but I left their home crying. I was not yet ready to take Danny out of my mind.

∞∞∞∞

I ran into Tony at the shopping plaza and I was lost for words. I think both of us were lost for words. I had parked the Benz in the parking lot and was getting ready to step out when he pulled up beside me in a Lincoln Navigator with three other men. I had seen Tony around before Danny's death, but I had never had reason to converse with him. His presence that day intimidated me and the men with him made it worse. They seemed like some blood hounds protecting their food. I pulled my car door in so that they could get out of their vehicle. As soon as I stepped out of my car, Tony came toward me and said, "You are Danny, the club owner's wife, right?"

I held my head up in the air, breathe deeply and said, "Yes, is there something I can help you with?"

"Yeah you might be able to. Me and Danny had some unfinished business discussions that I might need your help with."

I looked straight into his eyes and said, "A grieving widow might not be the best person to discuss business with. I would suggest that you give her time to get it together before trying to involve her in any business deals."

"Well, how much time do you need?" He sounded really arrogant and in control.

"You will know when I am through grieving," I responded.

What I really wanted to say was, the day I put a bullet in your head, I will stop grieving.

"Bubbler, try and stay out of his way. He is not a nice person, I am telling you. His family owns this entire town and he can easily get rid of you," the bouncer advised me when I told him I ran into Tony at the shopping plaza.

"Just like how he got rid of Danny," I said.

The bouncer cupped his head in his palm and looked like he regretted giving me any information. I touched him on his shoulder and said, "Don't worry I won't involve you in anything. I am going to handle everything on my own when the time is right."

∞∞∞∞

I went to Kingston to spend a couple of days and I went by my grandmother's house. It was great seeing everyone. It was always fun just hanging with them and listening to all the crazy things they talk about. My aunts knew everything that went on our street: who was sleeping with who; who was getting their asses whooped; who was knocked up by who; who had gone to prison; who had gone to foreign … and the list went on. Just sitting on the bench around the back of the yard as they talked nonstop and even quarrelling with each other about whose version was correct, made me miss having them around.

They said, Chris, Trina's old boyfriend had turned into the neighborhood's sugar daddy. All the young girls were flocking to him for his parents' money that he was squandering. They said the girls were fighting over him, but one day two friends teamed up and beat his ass when they found out he was sleeping with both of them.

"He is such a God damn fool," my cousin laughed.

"The Chinese boy isn't worth anything. The young girls beat the crap out of him. You should see his face, he looked like he wanted to cry," my aunt said. We all rolled over and laughed.

While being around my family took my mind off Danny, it fueled my quest to get revenge for his death. Being in my old neighborhood and hearing the stories and remembering that in order to survive you have to put all fears aside and be tough spurred my adrenaline for getting even. I thought about engaging one of my cousins who had somehow become one of the area leaders to see if he could assist me. But when I sent to call him and he came puffing on a joint and slinging a gun across his shoulder, I realized that I would be signing my own death sentence if I got him involved. He would probably just walk right up to Tony and his crew and it would be a shootout. No, I could not include any crazy in this situation. I had to do what I was doing on the low.

Momma pampered me the whole time I was at her

house. She kept telling me that I should forgive the guys who took my husband's life and try to move on with mine. Sophia had been in her ears trying to get her to convince me to give up the club and come to stay with her in New York. I kept telling Momma that New York was not the place for me, but she thought that I could at least start my life over there and then move to somewhere else once I get sorted out. I did not care about that, I just needed to deal with Tony and then decide on what direction I was taking with my life.

∞∞∞∞

I started going around the shopping mall more hoping to see Tony in order to figure out his movements. He was always surrounded by his blood hounds and sometimes some skinny, long-legged Indian girls with their behinds stuck up in their backs. They would flash their long hair around as they smiled up into his face. Twice he approached me about when I think I would be ready to discuss the unfinished business he had with Danny and each time my response was the same, "I am not in the best frame of mind to discuss any business just yet. I am still mourning the death of my husband."

I knew eventually Tony's patience was going to run out and I would be his next target. I thought that he was probably giving me some time to avoid raising any eyebrows so soon after Danny's death. I assumed Danny should have been killed before the wedding ceremony and it would have been a done deal for Tony. He knew Danny's parents were not interested in any business he was involved in and would have quickly gotten rid of everything including the land. The punks were too late and so I stood between Tony and what he wanted–Danny's land and weed business. He did not know that I was not an easy force to reckon with or they would have killed me that day too.

The bouncer said that Tony was never going to give up. "He wanted to take control of that land and the weed business so badly he had Danny killed for it. Don't you think he will do the same with you? You know that's what he wants so just sell him the land. It isn't worth losing your life over," he said.

I was determined that Tony was not getting that land to buy. Before I sold it to him, I would rather leave Montego Bay and then pay my cousin and his friends to deal with him once I was no longer around.

CHAPTER
TWENTY-SEVEN

The nights were lonely, long and awful. I had one dream after the other and I could not sleep. By the time I fell asleep, the sun was up and I would sleep until it was time for me to go to the club. The bouncer had become a big help. In fact, everyone rallied around me and pulled their weight. The club was still making money and drawing crowds especially on the weekends so I wasn't too concerned about it. What occupied my thought everyday was getting even. I lived, breathed and thought about ways in which to get rid of Tony. Sex seemed to fly right out of my head until one day I went to the club and was told that a White man came there earlier in the evening asking if I still worked there.

"A White man? What does he looks like?" I asked Bert.

"Like all White men do—White," Bert said giggling.

He did not leave any number, but said he would come back another time. That night all I could think of was Greg. Was he really in Montego Bay and trying to find me? I wondered. After all those years, did Greg still remember me?

That night I had different kind of nightmares as Greg occupied my thoughts. I took out the vibrators I brought back from New York and started working magic with the tan-colored one. When I released, the tension built up inside of me seemed to subside. I cried myself to sleep. The next day, I went to the club earlier than usual hoping that the person would come again but no one came that day, or the next, or the next. I figured it might have been someone who Danny might have conducted business with in the past and heard about his death and dropped by.

∞∞∞∞

Trina and Rick took me to out to dinner for my birthday and we ran into Tony with a woman at the restaurant. They were sitting not too far from where we were and seeing him took my appetite away. As I picked at my food, Trina asked if I was okay.

"I am fine," I said.

"You don't look fine, Bubbler. I can't imagine what it's like for you to have lost Danny, but it's been a while now. You have to try and pull yourself together. Do you realize how much weight you have lost? It doesn't seem like you are eating. I am sure Danny would not want you to live like this."

"I agree," Rick said. "You probably need to find someone who you can go out with to ease your mind. You're going to have to face the fact that Danny is not coming back and you still have plenty of life."

I was not paying any attention to all that they were saying. My mind was on how I was going to kill Tony. He looked over at our table and his eyes locked with mine. Does he suspect that I know he is responsible for Danny's death? I wondered. The way he looked at me whenever he saw me around made me feel like he knew. And he always laughed as if he was taunting me. My jaw tightened as I clinched my teeth as anger suddenly overcame me. I had my gun in my purse. In fact, I carried it everywhere with me now. But I held my emotions in check, looked down at my plate and continued picking at my food.

∞∞∞

I went to the beach one afternoon hoping to take a dip and chill out in the mid-afternoon sun. I had not gone to the beach in a long while although it was just a few miles from where I lived. I laid on my back on a towel on the sand with my arms folded behind my head and my sunglasses on looking up at the sun. I must have dozed off because when I awoke I saw someone standing over me. I did not see where he came from or when he walked up to me. I grabbed my sunglasses off and looked into a pair of the greenest eyes I had ever seen. They belonged to Greg. I jumped up off the sand and just hugged him without any of us saying a word.

I was suddenly overcome with so much emotions, I started to cry. He just held onto me as if I would disappear if he let go.

"Greg! Oh my God, Greg!" was all I could say.

When I finally regained composure, we sat down on the sand and he began to talk.

"Mercedes, I have been trying to find you for over a year now. I wrote you letters. I came last year and went to the condo and was told that you weren't living there anymore.

Then I stopped putting money in the account for the rent. I went to the club that you said you worked last week and they would not give me any information about you. You seemed to have disappeared."

"I would say the same about you too. You only tried to call me once, only once and I didn't even get to talk with you."

"I literally had no phone access, and when I did get a chance the time difference made it difficult. Oh Mercedes, I missed you so much."

"I missed you too Greg, I really do. So much has happened in my life, but through it all, I never forgot about you. I still missed you."

Greg rolled over into the sand and laid on top of me. I parted my legs and allow his midsection to position against mine. I closed my eyes and blocked out everything around me: the hot sun beating down on us as we laid in the sand; the seagulls as they flapped their wings and cawed at each other as they tried to find food; the waves lapping against the shoreline and the occasional sound of cars passing by. At that moment, the only thing that mattered was feeling Greg's heart beating against mine. I wrapped my arms around his shoulders as I felt my body tightening. We laid on the sand holding onto each other as the sweat from our bodies trapped the sand as it moved across the beach propelled by a light breeze blowing. I was in heaven.

Greg was staying at a hotel several miles away and was in Montego Bay for two weeks and more than a week had already passed. I went right back to the hotel with him and as soon as we walked through the door of the room, our clothes were scattered on the floor. I called the bouncer and asked him to handle things at the club for me for a couple of days. I went home, packed an overnight bag and spent the next couple of days holed up in the hotel with Greg. He was now living in Washington, DC to be closer to his parents. He said that his father was not in good health and so he was there to help out his mother. The last night we spent together, he wanted to take me back to the United States with him.

"Mercedes, I miss you. Come with me, I will take care of you," he pleaded with me.

"I am so sorry Greg, I really can't. Not yet anyway. I need to tie things up here first."

"Okay, but I really need you with me," he said.

As good as it sounded, I was hell bent on making sure Tony paid before leaving Montego Bay. When Greg dropped me off at my house on his way to the airport, I wanted to run inside, throw some things in a suitcase and follow him. But I could not. We hugged and kissed and did not want to let go of each other. That night when he called to say he had reached safely, we talked until the phone battery died. I had not slept so well in many months.

∞∞∞∞

I told the bouncer that I was looking into migrating and asked if he was interested in buying the club. He did not have the money it valued, but I told him I would work with him and that he could begin to put the money together. He seemed a bit relieved that I was planning on leaving Montego Bay. I knew he was concerned about the punks' killing and disappearance and was worried that information would eventually lead to me.

Tony was still looming around and had not given up on trying to get me to discuss the unfinished business with him. The bouncer was very worried that it was just a matter of time before I would be next. I no longer left the club late at nights and if I did the bouncer would always make sure that my car was parked in the front of the building under the lights instead of its usual place around the back.

I told Momma that I was selling the house and would leave the car with her. Momma was happy that I was planning on leaving Montego Bay although I did not tell her about Greg. She thought I was planning on going to New York to stay with Sophia so I offered no information. I was not sure what her reaction was going to be when she learned that I was planning on living with a man who I had never mentioned before.

∞∞∞∞

Seeing Greg again and talking with him on the phone every night invoked a whole new person in me. I once again became alive. Trina even said that my ass had also come alive too—it had been revived. I stopped worrying so much about Tony and started seriously thinking of leaving. As Danny's father said, I still had a lot of living to do and so I was going to look forward to what was in store for me.

∞∞∞∞

One night as I was leaving the club and heading home, I saw a car jumping in and out of lane. I veered away from it and kept a close distance behind. Based on the actions of the

driver, I assumed he was either intoxicated or high on
something. The car continued zigzagging up the street and
then it swung off the road and into an embankment. I pulled
up beside it and looked to see if the driver was okay and was
so shocked to see that it was Tony. He was all alone. He was
conscious enough to recognize me by the look on his face. I
quickly grabbed my gun out of my handbag and sent a shot
through his forehead. He slumped forward facing the wheel
and I put two more shots into his back and drove away. I
drove home hoping that no one saw my car driving away
from his vehicle. Everyone in the area knew I drove a black
Benz and we were on a busy main road.

The next morning, Tony's shooting was all over the
television news channels. Someone passing by noticed the car
in the ditch and stopped to look. After seeing the body
slumped over the wheel, they called the police. According to
the news, there were no clues as to what had happened and
the police were asking anyone who might have seen or heard
something to come forward. Tony's parents had even
initiated that they were willing to offer a reward to anyone
with information on the death of their son. As I watched his
mother crying on television and his father comforting her, I
was reminded of Danny's parents when they witnessed him
bleeding to death on his wedding day. I felt no remorse for
Tony's parents.

Trina called me and said, "Bubbler, turn on your
television."

"I already have the TV on, what is it?"

"Did you see the news with the businessman they found
murdered in his car?"

"Yes, I am watching the news report," I answered as

calm as possible. I didn't want to create any concern.

"What is going on? First Danny and then they found that taxi man on the beach and now this man. Rick needs to watch himself. It seems like someone is going around killing people."

I wanted to tell her that Rick didn't have anything to worry about. He had already learned his lesson from spending time in prison in America and all he talked about was not doing anything to lose his freedom again. Whenever I heard him talk, I would get nervous and try to push Danny to let go of his weed business. I had feared for his life and his freedom and my greatest fears were realized. Trina interrupted my thought as she asked, "Have you heard anything from the police regarding Danny's killers?"

"Nope, nothing at all," I told her.

∞∞∞

I called Greg and told him I was booking my ticket for Washington, DC. He was so excited, he said he would not mind if I was on the next flight out of Jamaica. That was all I wanted to hear. I was not going to wait around for anyone to hold me responsible for Tony's murder. Furthermore, I had nothing more in Montego Bay.

I went to St. Elizabeth to tell Danny's parents that I was leaving for good this time. Our final parting was very emotional. I could not help but shed some tears when Danny's mother hugged me before I left. Thelma's girls were also sad to see me leave. Everyone pretty much realized that this might be the last contact I would have with them for a long time, if not forever. I was moving on with my life.

I backed out of their driveway and headed toward Montego Bay and then decided to turn back and drive down the other direction. I passed Damion's mother house with the hope of getting a final glimpse of him. He was not outside playing and I did not have the courage to go knocking on his mother's door. Not seeing Damion, I turned around and headed home. Although I really wanted to see him, in a way it was a good thing I did not. Damion looked so much like Danny and seeing him would have caused me to start crying again.

∞○○○∞

When I handed the bouncer the paperwork for the club and took what money he had, I didn't have to tell him my task was accomplished—he already knew.

"Everything's good with you?" he asked.

"Yeah, everything's fine."

"Take care of yourself and keep in touch."

"I will. You take care of yourself too."

I gave him a hug, then I walked away and wiped the tears rolling down my eyes.

The next day I had my cousin and his friends empty everything from my house and load them into a moving truck to take to Kingston. I swung by Trina and Rick to tell them goodbye and headed to Kingston with two suitcases in the back of my car. I gave the keys to the house to Momma and told her to put it on the market. She would have no problem since it was in her name. I also gave her the keys and the title for the Benz and she dropped me off at the airport.

"Take care of yourself now. And call me as soon as you reach," Momma said.

"I will, Momma. You take care too."

I knew she was happy that I was leaving and I was too. I boarded a flight to Washington, DC with no any plans on returning to Jamaica anytime soon.

∞∞∞∞

The first night I spent with Greg in DC, he made me feel like I belonged with him. He met me at the airport with a bunch of flowers and literally lifted me up off the ground in the air. He could not wait to get home to have me in his arms. Red roses were scattered over the bed and a bottle of champagne was chilling on the side table. I did not have time to smell the roses much less to pour the champagne. He threw my big ass on the bed and we made love for hours.

The next morning as I unpacked, I saw the red negligée I had carefully picked out at a store in New Kingston with thoughts of dressing sexy and teasing Greg, but he didn't need any of that. If I had changed into it he probably would not have even noticed. He just wanted to get right down to business. I smiled as I caught his eyes staring at me from across the room. He smiled back and I got up and bundled up in bed with him. There was no rush in unpacking, I was there to stay.

Lying on top of Greg, I noticed for the first time that my chocolate-brown skin did not seem like it belonged against his white body–both looked so different. But for the moment that did not matter, our hearts beat as one. I knew that our love for each other was unbreakable. After all those years carrying Greg in my mind, I felt as if my soul belonged with him. I didn't know what life was going to be like living with him in a new country, but I was willing to give it my all. I had no intention of running away again.

I believe that love bubbling inside will spread and conquer all!

A Love Bubbling Inside

Sequel to Champion Bubbler

A novel

JULES MITCHELL BAILEY

Chapter 1

In the middle of the night, I found myself waking up screaming and asking God for mercy. I was tormented and could not sleep. I thought I had left all my troubles in Jamaica, but they seemed to follow me. Every night I was reminded of Danny's shooting and the revenge I took on those responsible for taking his life. In my dreams, the faces of his killers taunted me. The last contact I had with them was etched into my memory. My nightgown would be soaked with sweat that seeped from my pores. I would be in a state of shock as my body convulsed from the nightmares.

Greg would hold me in his arms and gently rock me like a child until the intensity of the dreams dissipated and I calmed down. He was lost for words and could not understand what was happening. How could he? He had no idea of what my life had been like when I lived in Jamaica or why I was so willing to leave. All he knew was that he met a woman who he thought he could not live without. He was fascinated with the curves of her body and the radiance of her chocolate-brown skin. And when he made love to her, she seemed to take him to places he had never been before. He was as eager to be with me as I was excited to be with him, but he had no idea of the secret life I had lived in Jamaica and all the things I was involved in with Danny.

As much as I was happy to be with Greg, I still missed Danny and was saddened by the way in which his life ended. I wondered what life would have been like if I had gotten the chance to live with him as his wife and to bear his children. I missed his parents, too.

Danny's mother was a petite Chinese woman with slanted eyes, a smooth olive complexion, and long black hair billowing past her waistline. And when she silently stared at me, her eyes seemed to telegraph through my brain, trying to figure out what my thoughts were. It was obvious that she loved her son very much and she wanted to confirm that the woman he had brought home was right for him. But despite her stare, she was warm and gracious and would ensure that I was comfortable while visiting her home.

Danny's father towered over his wife at over six feet, sporting a strapping build and a midnight complexion. It was clear that he liked talking with me when Danny and I visited. One day Danny joked, "It looks like Daddy is about to win you over. I need to step up my game."

I busted out laughing.

"Do you see how he is always trying to charm you?" he asked.

"Please, boy. Your father is an old man now, and he likes having conversations with me," I told Danny.

"Oh yeah, I am going to have to keep a close eye on both of you," Danny said as he winked.

I remembered that I had bent over and kissed Danny on

the cheek, and he looked at me and smiled. Now, living in Washington, DC, it felt like my world had been turned upside down. Every day I was tormented by memories of my life with Danny, my interaction and close connection with his family, and the hurt and pain I still felt because of his death.

This situation was taking a toll on my relationship with Greg, who (I thought) was not aware of my past life with Danny. While having to deal with the nightmares that woke him out of his sleep, Greg was also dealing with me not fully giving myself to him. While my body yearned for him, I was not in the frame of mind to satisfy his sexual needs. Greg suggested that I see a therapist.

"Mercedes, you cannot continue like this. You need someone to talk with. A therapist will be able to figure out what is going on, in order to help you," he said.

"I have never been to a therapist. I don't know what to expect."

"Don't worry about that right now. Let's focus on finding someone to help you. I don't know what is bothering you, and it doesn't seem like you want to talk with me, so let's find someone whom you can talk with."

I agreed, and so Greg started searching for a therapist. He found one who he thought might be able to help me work through my issues. He said he would pay for the services, but I refused. I had converted the money I had received from selling the club Danny left me into U.S. dollars and had deposited it into a foreign currency bank account. I had more than enough money to pay for the help I needed.

Greg was surprised that I had access to so much money, but he didn't question where I got it. So I decided to volunteer the information.

"I was earning good money in Jamaica and saved quite a bit. I also sold everything I had before I came here.

"I see," was all he said.

∞∞∞∞

I sat in the room, waiting on the doctor, and as I looked around, I noticed she had a picture on her desk with two children–a boy and a girl–and another picture with what I assumed to be her and her husband. On the walls were several diplomas, professionally framed. The one that caught my eyes read "Hyacinth Patrice Hines, MD, Johns Hopkins School of Medicine."

Dr. Hines, a tiny woman no more than five feet tall, walked into the office, smiled, and asked how I was doing.

"Not good," was my response.

"Tell me what is going on with you," she said as she sat behind the big, cherry wood desk, facing me.

I began to tell her that I could not sleep during the night as I was tormented with dreams of things that had happened in my past. I did not want to be specific, and she realized that, and shifted the conversation. She asked me to tell her about my family. She also wanted to know what it was like growing up. I began to talk about Momma and the many sugar daddies she had entertained while I was growing up. I told her I did not know who my father was because Momma never said, and I never asked. I talked about leaving Kingston to dance in a strip club in the tourist area of Montego Bay and about my relationship with the club owner, Danny, who was killed on our wedding day.

I could not control my emotions as the tears flowed

freely down my face. She handed me a box of tissues and gave me time to tell her everything I wanted to share before interrupting me.

"Were Danny's killers caught?" she asked.

How could I tell her that I personally took the lives of those responsible for his killing; hence, this was one of the reasons I left Jamaica after reconnecting with Greg? How could I tell her that every night the faces of Danny's killers tormented me, as their last expressions never left my memory? How could I tell her that I was still heartbroken about Danny, but was living with another man who I also felt I could not live without?

When I did not respond, she asked, "Are you afraid that Danny's killers are going to come after you?"

"They can't," I answered in a hushed voice.

I stared blankly at her for a few seconds without saying anything. She sat staring at me in anticipation that I would continue talking.

"Even if they could, I am not in Jamaica anymore, and I am not going back anytime soon. They can't hurt me," I said, looking straight into her eyes without showing any emotion.

While Danny's killers could not hurt me physically, they were tearing me apart. Greg was very concerned and I was not sure how much longer he was going to deal with my nightmares.

Dr. Hines recommended that I take medication to help me deal with my emotions and to sleep at nights. She also suggested that I see a counselor to help me work through some of the issues that I had bottled up inside. Dr. Hines gave me a recommendation for a counselor and a prescription for a thirty-day medication and said I should return to see her once I was finished taking the medication.

She wanted to do an evaluation to determine if the medication was working.

After taking the medication for a few days, I was stunned by the results. For the first time in more than a year, I was able to sleep peacefully. Greg was happy too, but I decided that I was going to go ahead and schedule an appointment to meet with the counselor. While taking the medication was a great quick fix, I knew my issues were deeper than what I was experiencing, and I wanted to get to the root of my problems.

This novel is available for purchase from:

- Amazon.com
- Amazon Europe (Amazon.co.uk, Amazon.de, Amazon.fr, Amazon.it, and Amazon.es.)
- CreateSpace eStore (https://www.createspace.com/championbubbler)

∞∞∞∞

To contact the author send an email to:
julesmitchellbailey@gmail.com

∞∞∞∞

To connect with the author on social media:

Like her Facebook page at:
https://facebook.com/julesmitchellbailey

Follow her on Twitter at:
https://twitter.com/juleselbailey

Follow her on Instagram at:
https://instagram.com/julesmitchbailey